DEATH IN DEIÀ

By the same author

Half a Pound of Tuppenny Rice

DEATH IN DEIÀ

by

DAVID COUBROUGH

GALILEO PUBLISHERS, CAMBRIDGE

First published by Galileo Publishers © 2019
16 Woodlands Road, Great Shelford, Cambridge,
UK, CB22 5LW

www.galileopublishing.co.uk
Galileo Publishers is an imprint of Galileo Multimedia Ltd.

ISBN 978-1-903385-86-9

Cover painting by Victoria Coubrough

Cover design by NamdesignUK

Character illustrations by Phil Cooke

Printed in the UK by TJ International
2 4 6 8 10 9 7 5 3 1

For Victoria, Olivia, Alice,
Emily and Jonathan

PROLOGUE

A s she walked along the landing towards the grand staircase with only her phone to light the way she noticed, as if for the first time, the portrait of her grandfather. It was hanging where it had always been, at the top of the stairs. He was seated, wearing a lounge suit, a brandy glass in one hand and a cigar in the other. His gaze was enigmatic; his penetrating blue eyes fixed on a point beyond the viewer. As she looked more carefully there seemed to be an anger, an unease and perhaps even a hint of insanity. She hurried down the stairs and ran across the cold hallway, her bare feet chilled by the marble floor.

The fetid aroma of Horace's cigars from earlier in the evening hung heavy in the air. The grandfather clock struck one am. She went over to the plastic bag she'd left on a side table earlier in the evening and took out three carrots and a mince pie, which she then carefully placed in front of the flickering fire. She enjoyed the warmth coming from it. It all felt so magical that for a moment she actually believed Father Christmas *would* be coming to enjoy his mince pie.

She was shaken from her reverie when she noticed that the presents, which had been so neatly stacked under the Christmas tree, had been disturbed and when she looked more closely she saw that many of them had been unwrapped. She flicked the light switch on the wall, but the light didn't come on. She knew there must be some perfectly rational explanation for all this, but even so felt a cold tremor of fear. A floorboard creaked but this was an old house which often rattled and sighed, so she tried to retain her composure. Suddenly she was brutally seized from behind and dragged backwards to the fireplace.

CHAPTER ONE

Grant Morrison climbed out of the air-conditioned taxi into the balmy warmth of the midday Mallorcan sun. He stretched his long legs. They were stiff from the lack of room in the back of the car. He had spent the forty minute ride from the airport to Palma Nova trying to get comfortable and trying to avoid talking to the driver. According to the ID tag dangling on the rear-view mirror, his name was Manolo and he was keen to practise his English, but Grant was in no mood for chit chat about why he had come, where he had come from and who was going to win the World Cup. He had pulled out his newspaper and Manolo had switched on the radio. The voices sounded tinny and hectic and did nothing to calm Grant's nerves.

Manolo was quick to open the boot and dump Grant's luggage on the hot pavement. Grant tugged his wallet from his back pocket and pulled out a fifty Euro note. He nodded, "Keep the change." Grant stared up at the large apartment block that loomed above him. He pulled a crumpled piece of paper from his pocket but realised that although he had the right address, he didn't have the actual number of the apartment.

He couldn't believe he'd been so stupid and stood on the pavement not sure what to do next. His only option was to ring random door bells and hope that whoever answered could speak English. His Spanish was rudimentary and he really didn't fancy trying to explain what had happened to a Spaniard at the other end of an intercom. He rang three different numbers. No one was in. Like a child he pressed his nose to the frosted glass door and spotted a small dark shape on the inside. He rattled the door and the shape got bigger as it moved towards him. It was the cleaner and she had abandoned her bucket and mop to open the door from the inside. Her brown, mousy hair hung like flat strips of fern on either side of her face.

"Carmen. I'm sorry to bother you. I'm looking for a friend, Mrs Alison Galvin." He had spotted the woman's name on a small, yellow badge stuck on her right lapel. She took a step backwards, looking nervous. "Do you know where I can find her?" She pointed to a bank of small wooden letter boxes attached to the left-hand wall. Grant quickly went over to inspect them. Frowning in concentration, he scanned the boxes. There were so many and all the names were hand written and hard to read. Then he saw it – Mrs A Galvin. The box was overflowing with envelopes and junk mail and obviously hadn't been opened for a very long time. Seeing the number seventy-seven on her box, he hurried back outside to press the buzzer on the console. No answer. Carmen disappeared into the lift. Frustrated, he stood staring at the seventy-seven buzzer, wondering how long it had been since it was last pressed. Had Mrs Galvin actually lived at number seventy-seven? Had she lived there alone? Had she lived there long? Had she lived there at all?

Distracted by a sudden clatter of crockery from the café next door, Grant decided to have a coffee and figure out what to do next. The owner was a small, friendly-looking man wearing a short-sleeved white shirt and black trousers that finished well short of his socks. He led Grant to a table with a red and white table cloth and a white plastic chair.

"Café solo por favor."

The owner nodded, dusted some sugar off the table and went to get the coffee.

Taking small sips of his scalding café solo, Grant sighed. He hadn't anticipated being frustrated so early on in his search. He beckoned to the owner and carefully took out of his wallet a tired and slightly cracked old polaroid picture of Alison Galvin and handed it over. He thought he saw a slight frown as the man stared at the photograph.

"You know the lady, yes?" Grant scrutinised him, waiting for a response. He narrowed his eyes as he studied the photograph. Alison Galvin was dressed in her Mary Quant coat, buttoned up to the top of her neck and was wearing horn rimmed glasses. Grant relaxed a little, sensing that she seemed familiar to the man.

"Ah, yes, she always has top button done up on blouse, but no, is now grey and looks . . ."

"Yes, my friend, this was thirty years ago, but we're talking about the same lady?"

The owner fell silent.

"Can you tell me about her. Please?" Grant's urgency surprised the man and he looked confused.

"I think," he said.

"Yes?"

"I think, she is lady who disappeared." The owner looked frightened and quickly turned away.

"Just a moment!" Grant's voice rose, "How? When?"

"You ask wrong man, Mister. I only see her with gentleman friend, come in for coffee and smoke."

"But why no more?"

The owner turned back to face the unwanted customer. "No

person know, but they said she *dead* . . ."

Dead? Grant could hardly believe it, but that would, of course, explain the pile of letters in the apartment block. He ordered another coffee and began to think about the Galvins. He knew how the family had splintered: the father, Paul, had been beaten down by financial failure and died prematurely, a broken man. Alison, his widow, had manipulated her father, the outrageously wealthy Ken Stone, on his death bed, and swindled her sisters out of their inheritance. So where was Alison Galvin? Was she really dead? Before he came to Mallorca he had phoned her son, Danny. The conversation had not gone well: "Why are you looking for her? What's your game now?" Grant took a deep breath, telling him he only wanted to pick his mother's brains about buying property in Mallorca, reminding him he knew she had bought a house there. Or had she? Glancing up he saw the café owner back in front of him.

"Mister, you don't look for old lady!" His voice had a menacing edge. "You go now please. Mister!"

"Who instructed you to tell me that?"

The man scowled, stepped back from the table and walked quickly to the kitchen. Grant stayed at the table for a while, lost in thought, trying to make sense of what he had just heard. Things were beginning to feel sinister and a nagging feeling of dread took hold. He leaned forward with his hands on his knees and his thoughts turned to the other person he very much wanted to find.

He paid the bill and hurried away. As he turned the corner he hit his shoulder with a painful jolt on a lamppost and his suitcase tipped over backwards as he dropped its handle. He cursed aloud and was sweating in the oppressive midday heat. He spotted a Car Hire sign across the road and decided the best thing would be to drive to his hotel in Deià and not waste any more time in Palma Nova.

He took the long, twisting coastal route and drove through olive and citrus groves. There was no traffic and he was beginning to unwind, taking in the views and letting his mind wander back to happier times. It was here, over twenty-five years earlier, that he had met a dazzling, dope-smoking Australian woman who had offered him the chance of a heady freewheeling life in Mallorca. When she reached out to him for help, he had taken fright and scuttled back to his respectable life in the Home Counties. He had been haunted by his cowardice ever since.

Suddenly something large was in front of the car. He braked and swerved, skidding towards the steep drop down to the sea. The car stopped inches from a gap in the boulders which had been placed haphazardly on the cliff. He was trembling and sweating and looked back to see an elderly billy goat wandering away down the hill. He reversed back on to the road and gradually his composure returned. Eventually the road became wider and he relaxed a little. Breathing more easily, he took in the view of isolated fincas and cemeteries, almond trees arranged in terraces, pine woods and yet more olive groves. Annoyingly, a car was now behind him which meant he couldn't meander along in quite the way he would have wanted but eventually he found himself driving down towards the beautiful seaside town of Sant Elm. Turning right into a bumpy car park he squeezed between two trees and parked. He strolled up the hill and soon found a ramshackle street café, where car fumes floating on the warm summer air were no more than a minor irritation. He was pleased to be alive. He looked back at the car park and noticed the car that had been behind him, a grey Citroën, was also parked there.

Gazing out to sea, he narrowed his focus, spotting what looked like a monastery on top of a small island. He wondered about the people who had lived there down the ages – Carthaginians, Romans, Muslims from the North African invasion of the Middle

Ages. He had read about the Arabs who had brought crops and introduced irrigation systems. He was aware of the struggles with other
European nations and how the peace was constantly threatened by
pirate ships in the sixteenth and seventeenth centuries. Reflecting on
the ruined watchtowers that dotted the landscape he thought of his
own life; one minute everything is fine and the next everything is
upended. Nothing remains comfortable for long.

Searching for messages on his mobile, he frowned as he thought
more about Alison Galvin. Where was she, how could she just
disappear and what did the café owner know? He recalled again how
she'd ripped off her sisters, taking all their inheritance, before running
off to start a new life among the other 100,000 Brits on Mallorca.
But someone must know what had happened to her. He stared out
at the calm blue sea stretching out in front of him. But he also knew
that all this Galvin stuff was just a pretext for him to be here. He was
interested in someone much more important than Alison Galvin.

A text from an old friend, Justyn Silver, startled him, *What are you
up to?* Justyn, the one friend from the past who had always supported
him, was now asking questions. Grant wondered how Justyn knew
he was in Mallorca. He decided to ignore the text for now. Back in
the car, he glanced in his rear mirror and saw the same grey Citroën
he'd spotted at Sant Elm.

As he climbed the twisting mountain roads with the warm air
coursing through the open windows, Grant drank in the dramatic
landscape and the clear, sharp light. He gloried in the occasional aristo-
cratic Spanish house, dappled in late afternoon sunlight, bougainvillea
covering the gateway and surrounded by brightly coloured begonias.
He drove on through Banyalbufar towards Valldemossa. Then he
turned left towards Deià.

He finally arrived at the hotel which was nestled beneath a craggy
mountain and his eyes were drawn down a valley to a rugged coast

with blue sea. The bucolic tinkling of sheep bells and explosive honking of burros higher up in the mountains were accompanied by the noise of motor engines and light building excavations from across the valley – both now permanent features of the island. Relieved to see he had a signal on his phone, he stayed in the car and called Justyn.

"Okay señor, so what's the big deal?"

"Grant, I've no idea exactly what you're up to, but Danny's not at all happy. He's thinking about coming over too."

"He's got nothing to fear from me. His Mum's gone missing, so's her companion. Would've thought he'd be very keen to find out …"

Justyn was silent for a moment.

"How much do you know about his mother?"

"Only that she ripped off her sisters and disappeared to a new life in Mallorca."

"Why does she concern *you*? I think you'd do well to mind your own business. You don't want to get mixed up in this!" Grant was deciding how to respond, when Justyn surprised him by calmly announcing that he was coming to join him.

"What the hell's going on Justyn? Why're you coming out? And by the way, there's something you should know."

"What?"

"It sounds ridiculous and I may be a bit paranoid, but I think I may have been followed on the journey here to Deià."

"That doesn't surprise me. Grant, you're playing a dangerous game. Why are you really on your own in Mallorca, and what are you doing in Deià?"

"Can't say on the phone. I'm looking for someone. I'm staying at the Hotel Villaverde."

The line went dead. Grant saw the Citröen again in the car park and this time a couple was standing next to it.

★★★★★

Grant checked in at the hotel; a friend had told him of its charm. It was an old Mallorcan house converted into a small family hotel with wonderful views of the mountains – and it wouldn't break the bank. He was escorted to his room by a tall young receptionist. He was struck by her short dark hair and beautiful olive skin. He had a strange feeling that he had met her somewhere before. She seemed not so much to walk, as float down the corridor towards his room. As she turned the key in the door their eyes met. He noticed that her eyes were the same colour as his, green. Embarrassed he looked away, unable to think of anything to say. The girl handed him the key.

"If there's anything you need, please call Reception." She gave a weak, uncertain smile and closed the door behind her. He opened it again and called after her.

"Just one thing." He paused, but seeing her scurrying away thought better of it. "Oh, nothing."

"If you think of it, call Reception." Her tone was at once professional, though wary. She hurried down the stairs. This man troubled her; she returned to the desk and stood fretting, trying to fathom why. She didn't think he'd looked at her in an inappropriate or lustful way – she was familiar enough with that – no, this man had viewed her with some kind of recognition. In the evening, she watched him go out. He placed his key respectfully on the reception desk but didn't speak or look up.

★★★★★

Two days later when Leia went into Grant's room to help one of the housekeeping girls, she found the bed had not been slept in. The room had been tidied the previous morning and, apart from a bulky manila folder on the desk, had a vacant look. She thought she should speak to her boss, Sergio.

"Leia?" Sergio, the owner – a squat, bedraggled looking man – glanced up from his hunched position behind the desk. She knew he appreciated her contribution to his hotel; she worked hard and never complained about anything he asked her to do. He'd told her on more than one occasion that he saw her as a possible part of the hotel's long term future as he needed to 'wind down'. This was good news for her as she was worried about her own future. The Melias, who owned the main village store, had kindly given her lodgings above their shop when her mother died, when Leia was only fourteen. In return she helped them in the shop. She enjoyed working there but was concerned that the Melias, who were now in their eighties, were talking about selling up. She feared this would include her flat. She appreciated that they had recommended her to Sergio. She was determined to impress him.

"It's señor in Room five, he has not returned to his room. It looks as if he's not been back since yesterday morning."

Sergio nodded to himself, then lifted his eyes to the ceiling.

"Leia, this happens quite a lot actually. People check in for a few days and don't necessarily come back every night. We still charge them." He looked dismissively out of the window.

"Yes, but this guy…"

"What? What about this guy? Why is he different to all the other bozos we get, all the drifters, all the adventurers? Why is he any different?"

"Well I don't really know but he's weird, in fact I'd say he's very strange." She began to blush.

"So what's so strange?"

"He's really freaked me. The way he looked at me. His eyes drilled right through me." Sergio remained seated and pushed his glasses up the bridge of his nose. He knew Leia was going beyond her remit, giving her opinion of a random guest, but decided against reprimanding her. Tapping on his computer, he soon found the absent man's details.

"Grant Morrison." He cast a watchful eye on Leia but she just shrugged. The name clearly didn't register.

"I'm sorry, I've wasted your time." Leia sprang to her feet, backing out of the office, wishing she hadn't even mentioned it.

"Don't worry about it. I know you're concerned Leia but I'm sure he'll turn up."

★★★★★

After leaving the hotel, Grant drove to Sóller. He loved this place, nestled in the heart of the Valley of Oranges and achingly picturesque, with its cobbled streets and terracotta roofs. This was where, twenty five years earlier, he had first met Angie. She was working in a dilapidated bar near where he was staying. When he first saw her she was wearing a gypsy skirt, with a low slung belt and a little white top. The straps were pulled down showing her brown shoulders and she wore her long, dark hair in a loose plait. She was warm and vivacious and so unlike the women he usually spent time with. He found himself going to the bar more and more often.

He was between jobs and had decided to spend the whole summer in Mallorca in a friend's flat. At first he had thought it was all a terrible mistake – he was lonely and not a very good tourist. But then he met Angie. They spent lots of time together. She took him all over the island. They swam, hiked in the mountains, smoked dope, drank cheap red wine and made love in her tiny bedsit. It was full of her paintings – huge, colourful canvases. He'd never understood abstract art so had no idea whether they were any good or not but he did know that he had never felt so happy or so free. There was talk of him staying. Perhaps he could get a job as a lawyer on the island.

But then came the terrible day when Angie announced that she was pregnant. The summer idyll was over. This was not what he wanted. Grant found an icicle in his heart. He gave Angie a cheque for five hundred pounds and told her to have an abortion. Three days later he flew back to England. He had regretted it ever since, but he also knew that back then he was too young and perhaps in the end, too conventional, to have stayed with Angie. For years he didn't know that she had kept the baby, but when she died, his friend, whose flat he had borrowed all those years ago, contacted him with the sad news and added in passing, that she'd had a fourteen year-old daughter. He didn't know the details and Grant felt a kind of emotional paralysis. He was shocked at the news, both that she had died and that her daughter might possibly be his. He longed to fly straight out then and there, but he was married and had no idea how to tell his wife. Again he fell back into his comfortable life but when, ten years later, he heard about the Galvin scandal, he decided that this would give him the perfect reason to visit the island again and perhaps even find his daughter.

And now here he was back in Sóller. He was keen to visit his old haunts to try and find out what had happened to Angie's daughter and perhaps even meet up with her although, given how badly he had behaved, he knew that she would probably not want anything to do with him. He went back to the bar where he had first met Angie, but it had been renovated and was unrecognisable. Then to the bedsit. But the whole building had been demolished and a block of flats was standing in its place. It was hopeless and depressing and he decided to go back to Deià.

★★★★★

Just as Grant was leaving Sóller a group of cyclists was gathering in the nearby town of Valldemossa. Their leader was Guy Roope, a large, bull-necked man with severely cropped chestnut-coloured hair. Since leaving the SAS a few years earlier, he had maintained peak fitness by obsessively working out. He had only taken up cycling a year earlier. It ticked all his boxes. It was a good shop window for showing off his physique and powers of endurance. He needed to be seen as an alpha male and the Bedford and Rural cycling club had proved the perfect showcase. Various charitable causes had been adopted for his different excursions but it never troubled him that he rarely remembered which cause he was cycling for.

The temperature was already up and the sky was clear, as he watched his twenty-strong group assemble noisily in Valldemossa's crowded high street. Guy, his face red from the previous day's cycling, marshalled them into two lines of ten.

"Remember only two abreast, nobody breaks ranks." He didn't so much announce as bark his instructions. The chattering stopped. The team knew better than to upset their organiser. They all knew his SAS background; they'd all learned to fear his mood swings.

A loud hooter announced the start. Obediently following their leader, with their hands tightly gripping the handlebars as if to stop them running away, the cyclists began to pedal furiously. With their humped backs and pointed helmets they looked like a flock of birds desperately trying to get up enough speed to take off. They followed the road as it snaked round hairpin bends before descending into Deià. Parked delivery vehicles slowed the pace through the narrow high street, but once through the town, they picked up speed and were soon on the vertiginous road towards Sóller.

Meanwhile Grant was not enjoying his drive. He had to concentrate hard on the narrow twisting road. He was leaning forward, gripping the wheel tightly and sweating profusely. When he realised that the air conditioning had stopped working, he pressed the switch to open all the windows but his momentary lack of concentration caused the car to swerve and he narrowly avoided knocking down an elderly man who was standing at the side of the road. Once past, he slowed down and, glancing in the wing mirror, was relieved to see two people hurrying to the man's aid. Startled by a motorcycle screaming round the corner behind him, he accelerated. Hot air was coursing through the car and he wiped sweat from his eyes with the heel of his hand. A coach, completing its own blind turn, gathered pace and bore down on him. From the other direction Guy Roope's cycling group hurtled downhill towards him, veering into the middle of the road as they turned. Grant pulled to the right and in the wing mirror he saw two cyclists gesticulating angrily back at him. Distracted, he skidded into a side gulley, where the tyres racked up against a water run; yanking the wheel hard left, he rejoined the road just in time to see a car racing down the hill towards him, its headlights switched to main beam. It was coming straight at him. He could make out two heads, the driver and passenger. He threw the wheel hard right and crashed into a low barrier hearing the rasping crunch of metal on metal. The car missed him by inches. He felt a sudden urge to contact Justyn but thought better of it. He decided to keep driving and to get off the road as soon as he could.

Back on the road he grew faint with shock. He was becoming weaker by the moment and his head was spinning. His hands gripped the wheel like the claws of an animal climbing a tree but as he began to lose consciousness, his grip slipped and the car swerved right. He knew his car was falling over the cliff, tumbling down the mountain slope, and he knew he would soon feel nothing at all.

*****

They found him two days later. A young *policia* had stopped at a gap in the bushes at the top of the hill and noticed some broken branches. He guessed that a car could have fallen through it. He stepped out of his vehicle, walked across to the gap, peered down and gingerly slithered down the mountain side. He was right. The car was some fifty feet below in the ravine with what looked like a body torpedoed through the windscreen. The young officer wiped the sweat from his brow and stared at the wreckage in front of him. He had found the man they had all been looking for.

CHAPTER TWO

Grant's body was laid out on a stainless steel table and covered by a white sheet. The mortuary attendant pulled back the sheet to reveal Grant's battered face. His hair had been neatly combed back revealing his receding hairline and Justyn smiled, knowing that Grant would not have been best pleased about that. There was a strong smell of soap and bleach and Justyn struggled to hold back the tears.

This was not the reunion with his old friend that he had anticipated when he decided to join him in Mallorca. The gashes on Grant's face had been neatly stitched, but instead of the deathly pallor that Justyn was expecting, Grant looked rather well. Some kind of concealer had been used to cover the extensive bruising and there was blusher on his cheeks. It was both ridiculous and utterly tragic. Justyn had never seen a dead body before. He had been to plenty of funerals but there was something so shocking about standing next to someone he knew so well, who was there but not there at all. Grant's eyes were closed and as Justyn struggled to cope with the fact that he would never speak to him again, he felt a light touch on his elbow, reminding him of his purpose there.

"Yes, that's Grant Morrison." He was ushered gently from the room.

He had been asked to identify the body by Grant's wife, Brigit.

She was far too distraught to travel.

His next errand for Brigit was to go to the Hotel Villaverde to pick up Grant's personal effects. The proprietor had cleared the room and packed Grant's bags. Justyn was grateful for that but realised that his kindness was of course expediency. He couldn't have a room left empty waiting for a guest who was never going to return. He offered his condolences and then reached under the desk.

"There is something else, senõr."

"Oh. What's that?"

"This folder was left on the desk in the room. We thought it should be kept separate as it seems to contain a lot of personal papers." He handed over a canvas bag with the logo of the hotel on the side and Justyn peered inside to see a mass of notebooks and loose paper.

"Thank you so much. I'll see that it all gets to his widow in the UK."

★★★★★

That night back in his hotel Justyn had drowned his sorrows with far too much Albarino and ended up jamming with the musicians who were playing in the bar. As a rebellious teenager he had left school to play in a band, much against the wishes of his parents and he still wore his hair long, even though it was now grey and thinning. He had been secretly nursing a nagging pain in his hip but couldn't face the fact that it was probably arthritic and would only get worse. He didn't plan to age gracefully.

The next morning he woke with a start and took a few hesitant steps into the bathroom. He hung his head over the sink, and slowly looked up at the mirror. He did not like what he saw. His hair was lank and greasy, his eyes were bloodshot and his skin looked dull and lifeless. As he turned away from the mirror and stripped off for a shower, his phone rang.

"Hi, it's me."

"Yeah, no, I mean, I can see it's you, it said so on the phone … huh."

"It's been six months, JS." A tingle of pleasure rippled down his spine. Clare was calling to remind him that their six month separation, suggested by their relationship counsellor, was now over. He felt heartened as she only called him JS when she felt affectionate.

"Yeah CL," replying in kind, "and how in the name of all good things are you?"

"Well, I was doing fine, but I've just heard about Grant."

"Yeah, I know it's such a shock!" He decided not to mention his visit to the mortuary.

"But where are you? The dialling tone tells me you're abroad?"

"Yeah. I'm in Deià actually, in Mallorca." He thought of holding back, but it wasn't really his style.

"Oh? Why?"

"Because I'm trying to find out," he hesitated, "to find out what happened to Grant; I spoke to him from England just before he died."

"You're there really quickly aren't you? Mum told me his accident was only reported two days ago?"

"Your mum? How does she know?" Clare fell silent.

"This is really weird, JS, but the police have arrested Guy."

"Guy? Who's Guy?"

"Guy Roope, my cousin, Aunt Diana's son. You've met him. I'm sure you have."

"Why've they arrested him?"

"He was cycling, in a large group of some sort. The *policia* have evidence that they passed Grant's car just before it careered off the road."

"Surely ..."

"I know he can't be involved. I mean why the hell would he want to cause an accident? But they've taken him in for questioning. His cycling group were the only people they identified as passing Grant on the journey."

"Weird." Justyn fell silent. He heard the phone line make a crackling noise. "How well do you know this Guy?"

"Well we got to know the Roopes a lot better after Aunt Alison screwed us all over, up to then we'd always seen more of the Galvins. Never really knew Guy's father – bit of a cold fish Mum always said – he left when Guy was about twenty. Guy always struck me as a bit strange."

"I remember him now, quite a remote sort of person. So let me get this straight. Grant comes to Mallorca, apparently tries and fails to find Danny's mum. Meanwhile this Guy Roope's on the island at the same time; Grant falls to his death off the road just after being passed by Guy and his bike riders. Now apparently Danny's on his way out."

"So am I."

"What?"

"I need to get to Mallorca too. I need to help Mum find Alison."

"I see. I mean good. Can we meet?"

"Of course."

Although Justyn was keen to see Clare, it seemed an inappropriate time to be rekindling what had been a rather fraught relationship. He had just too many things on his mind. Earlier in the day, he'd been startled to receive a text message from Grant: *So good to talk, will be great to meet up in Deià. I think I've spotted the person I'm looking for!* He now worried he would be on the police radar. He'd heard they had Grant's damaged mobile phone and knew he would soon receive a knock on the door. Almost on cue the hotel manager phoned his room to tell him that someone wanted to see him downstairs. As he headed down,

Clare called him again. He stopped on the landing to take the call.

"Hi."

"Hi again, just thought you should know Aunt Alison isn't where we all supposed her to be."

"Where was that?"

"In some apartment block near Palma."

" Grant found that out. He was looking for her. I know, you'd think it odd but it was all quite innocent apparently. He just wanted to pick her brains on buying property."

"And now he's dead. JS, be careful. Mum told me even Danny doesn't know where his mother is."

"So where did Danny think she was?"

"She told him she was in Palma Nova with her gentleman friend, who was president or something of the block where she was meant to be living. All a pack of lies. She said she was quite safe and happy and told him it was best if he and his sister Sharon didn't contact her. Told them they would receive their inheritance if everyone 'played ball'."

"So he's had no contact with his mother since she left the UK?" He heard footsteps coming up towards him.

"Apparently she contacted him and Sharon from time to time, saying all was good, all would be sorted, she couldn't wait to see them again, that sort of stuff. She came back to England and saw them every now and then. But never wanted them to go to Mallorca."

Justyn didn't reply. A young *policia* with a thick black moustache was now standing in front of him and ordered him in broken English to end his call and accompany him to the local station. Clare heard the commotion before the line went dead.

"Look, I've got rights you know, I want a lawyer."

"Te hemos estado esperando." Justyn glared back, displaying his reckless disdain for authority.

*****

A little earlier Guy Roope had also been taken in for questioning in Palma Nova. His broad frame barely fitted through the narrow turn-stile, as he was led into an interview room. There was a stench of disinfectant and vomit.

He could hear a noisy group banging on what he presumed to be cell doors. It wasn't hard to identify fellow Brits as they broke into a chorus of "You've All Gone Quiet Over There!"

"Did you know Grant Morrison?"

A Spanish interpreter, bald with a shiny scalp, translated, although the three officers who had taken him into custody all seemed fluent in English.

"I only heard of him this evening from my mother."

"And how about Justyn Silver?"

"What?" Guy squeezed his fists under the table.

"Or let's try Danny Galvin?" Guy shifted his backside in his chair. It was too small and added to his discomfort in this grim little room. His face was sunburnt after cycling for several days in the heat and as the questions started he felt his face becoming even more flushed. He knew he looked guilty, squirming in his chair and red in the face.

"Justyn is Clare Loosemore's boyfriend. Well, sort of boyfriend. And Clare is my cousin, and Danny Galvin's also a cousin." His voice almost whispered.

The three officers looked at each other with a growing sense of triumph. Their questions had been based on the details of Grant's last phone calls on his mobile. Nodding at each other, they had no intention of letting him know that.

"You see Mr Roope, we are intrigued to find you have relations on the island. We have to wonder about this, just as we do about your passing Mr Morrison in his car with your cycling team. Soon after this Mr Morrison falls off the road."

They all stared at him. He looked away and made to get up from his chair. His questioner held his hand out, palm down, motioning him to stay where he was. Guy shifted in his chair, unclenched his hands, and placed them flat on his thighs.

"These are just coincidences."

"Can we have your mobile phone?" Guy heard the sound of an incoming call: looking down, he saw it was from Horace Loosemore, Clare's brother. Instinctively he changed the mode to 'silent' and handed over the phone.

"We will need this for a while. Would you like a cup of tea?" Guy shook his head, watching the man leading the interrogation walk quietly out of the room.

The other two men followed him. Guy dropped his face into his hands. Having been confident he would be cleared of any involvement in anything, he was now not so sure. Who could he get to vouch for him? His cycling group would certainly endorse the fact that no car had veered off the road in their presence, none that they were aware of. He made a mental list of the people who could testify to his innocence, although of what he couldn't be sure. He worked it out that they must have Grant Morrison's mobile phone, and had been rifling through his messages. Relieved at this thought, he half-smiled feeling more confident as the lead interrogator and his translator re-entered the room.

"Mr Roope, who is Mr Horace Loosemore?"

"He's a cousin, as well, brother of Clare."

"We thought so."

"Why?"

"He leave you message." Guy stared at the text in disbelief. The officer continued, "Let me read it for you."

"Hi big boy, the net is closing. I'm on my way to join you, don't leave

Mallorca until we've NAILED THE BITCH." Guy flinched.

The *policia* fixed his stare at Guy, scrutinizing him carefully as if he expected him to make a run for it at any moment. But something wasn't right and he knew he couldn't detain him any longer. Rising to his feet, he grunted, "You're free to go, but we'll be watching you!" He left the room, neither looking back nor bothering to see Guy out.

*****

Horace Loosemore returned his plane seat to upright and called after the stewardess as she hurried past.

"Another gin, plenty of ice, don't bother with the tonic." She glanced down at the pile of miniature Gordons stacked in front of him and dutifully replenished his stock, smiling insincerely. "The stewardesses get prettier every flight!" Ignoring him was, she considered, the best option.

Horace had grown up seeing wealth made visible. No one else lived in a house like his Grandpa's. He recalled a huge, chauffeur-driven limousine collecting him and his cousin Guy, from primary school and whisking them off to the circus in London. Other parents waiting at the school gates watched in disbelief.

"It should have been ours!" he said out loud. The woman on his right cast him a disapproving glance. Ever since the will revealed Alison as the sole beneficiary of the three sisters, he had referred to that time as 'the day the balloon went up'. He leaned back in his seat thinking about how he was going to find his mother's sister. He smiled to himself as he envisaged success: how he would make her sign a 'Deed of Arrangement' to ensure a proper share of the spoils, how his mother would finally get her due, and how he, Horace Loosemore, would enjoy the good life for the rest of his days. "Fine wines, first class travel, a house on Mustique." He quietly slipped into a drunken stupor.

On arrival at Palma, he headed for the car hire queue and was aware of a small man standing very close behind him. Strangely, he noticed him again as he was driving away: he was standing on a corner and was picked up by a grey Citröen. Horace thought nothing more of it.

His sister, Clare, had alerted him to the drama unfolding in Deià and he called her to ask where she might be. He detected reticence. Clare seemed to have no idea where she was and didn't seem particularly thrilled when he suggested meeting up with her old flame, Justyn Silver.

Horace had worked in the City, on and off for some twenty years, but no one was really sure what he actually did. When asked, he would say 'he worked in bonds: could be Brook, could be James', which made everyone cringe. In reality everyone suspected he hadn't actually worked for years, but continued to go out telling his wife Annabel he had important meetings in the City. He would leave home in a suit only to meet old friends in a wine bar for lunch, and would still be drinking at nine pm. He'd get back drunk and dishevelled and Annabel would humour him and persuade him to go to bed, except for one famous occasion when she locked him in the garage all night. Recently he had boasted he was going to make their fortune dealing in 'Bitcoins.'

★★★★★

The detective leant on the table, impatient to start the interview with Justyn. He was holding a report of Guy Roope's interview in Palma Nova.

"Why were you talking to Grant Morrison just before he died?" His voice was brusque and as unpleasant as his thin, mean-looking lips. But Justyn was not to be cowed. He squared his shoulders and held the man's gaze.

"I'm not sure why I'm here." He looked around at the stark room, taking in the two unshaded lights. "I understand you are investigating an accident, in which, tragically, my good friend Grant Morrison died, and I think you should allow me a period of mourning ..." Justyn's face flushed with anger.

"Oh, do you?" the *policía*, who had been in the hotel when Grant's body was found, glared at him.

"You should know we have his mobile and all the phone records. The last call he ever made was to you. There are very good reasons why we now interview you." Justyn half turned away. He'd always challenged authority. He said nothing.

"If you don't speak, we'll have to charge you with perverting the course of justice."

"I want a lawyer. You manhandle me out of my hotel, hole me up here for several hours, hound me as if I'm a common criminal! One of my best friends has died and you interrogate *me!*"

"You should know why your friend, Mr Morrison – one of your best friends – " he added sarcastically, "had two conversations with you on the day he died. We are wondering whether he talked to you about someone we know has disappeared. Alison Galvin. We know she is meant to live in a block in Palma Nova with a friend. We now think she never lived there. We know Grant looked for her and that Mr Roope is her nephew."

"Who?"

"Mr Roope, Mr Guy Roope, who passed Mr Morrison with his cycling group on the Sóller to Deià road, just before he crashed."

Unsettled by this information, Justyn recalled Clare explaining who was involved, including Guy Roope, but decided to keep it to himself.

"Who is Horace Loosemore?"

"He's a friend of mine's brother."

"Clare Loosemore?"

"Yes."

"Quite a little family reunion we have going on now, Mr Silver. Your friend Clare, her cousin Guy Roope, and now Clare's brother, Horace Loosemore. It seems strange to us that you are all now here in Mallorca."

"Horace is here now?"

"He will arrive shortly at Palma airport."

Although Justyn felt anxious, he feigned indifference. As an interior designer, he could never resist wanting to redesign every room he entered. But this room was different. He had no interest in it whatsoever, and badly felt the need to get out of it.

"Look, I know there are things going on you need to investigate, I quite understand. But I can assure you I have no information that helps you with your enquiries. None."

CHAPTER THREE

Danny Galvin slowly paced around his car showroom. Outside the skies had opened, and water was pounding the pavement. "Should be in Mallorca, not stuck here," he said to no one in particular.

He was cursing the little local difficulty that had delayed his planned flight to Palma. The previous day had brought unwelcome visitors. Bailiffs acting on behalf of HMRC had swooped into his office and started seizing goods in lieu of unpaid VAT.

Cheryl, in reception, had buzzed on the intercom.

"Danny, there are some gentlemen here who say they've come to collect computers and stuff, say you've ignored all the warnings."

"What?" Danny hadn't waited for a reply. He jumped up from his desk, crossed swiftly to the showroom, and headed straight towards a bunch of tough looking individuals.

"Who the hell are you?"

"Who are we?" A big, burly man, with the neck of a boxer, towered over Danny, forcing him to move back a few steps.

"Alright, Guv, the game's up, somebody's not been paying his VAT." Danny tried to pull himself up to his full height and looked his aggressor straight in the eye. But he was powerless to intervene and could only watch as two 'heavies', their overalls barely covering the thick tattoos on their powerful arms, started to remove the furniture in reception.

"Just tell me what the devil you think you're doing."

"Come on boys. Time to take the goods and chattels."

"Wait, I'm sure there's a mistake."

"Oh yeah, and I'm about to be anointed as the new Pope! Look, you can see smoke coming out of that building over there! I've heard it all Guv, no doubt you'll tell me Elvis ain't dead and you're a close mate of Prince Charles, who's going to scuttle round here and vouch for your good character." He glanced at the others, who were all sniggering at him.

"Hang on!" Danny shouted, "Wait here will you, I'll make a phone call."

He called Head Office and asked for Rob Bailey, the financial controller, only to be told he didn't work there anymore; anxiously he asked for Gill Watson, Bailey's assistant, only to be told she'd also left. In desperation he called the direct line of the CEO, Ralph Stockdale, to be fobbed off with "It's an administrative error, calm down Danny, we'll sort it!."

Danny managed to persuade the heavies to leave, agreeing to a two-day moratorium, having put Stockdale on the phone to the head honcho. Danny fell back into the chair in reception, hurriedly taking the medication he kept permanently in his jacket pocket as an insurance against panic attacks. He wondered, not for the first time, why he had ever sold his company to these cretins. He knew his company had paid the quarterly VAT payments to the parent company. Why had they neglected for three quarters not to pass it on to HMRC? He knew the answer: rumours were rife that the parent company was in trouble. He wished now he hadn't agreed to stay on, but what really disturbed him was the fact that VAT fraud had brought his father a short, unwanted stay at Her Majesty's leisure. He now wouldn't be able to fly out to Mallorca until this was all sorted out. He knew others were now gathering: Justyn was already there and his Aunt Pat had told him her son, Horace, was on his way and Horace's sister, Clare, was just about to go. His conversation with his Aunt Pat had unnerved him, and he knew he was probably unwise to ring his other aunt, Diana. But now everyone was getting involved he felt he had to talk to them. The conversation with Diana did not start well:

"You've got a cheek ringing me, young Danny, after what's happened!" He didn't expect much else but couldn't help half smiling at the epithet young, given he was well into middle age.

"I know, but things really aren't what you think."

"So what are they?"

"It's Mum … she's vanished!"

"Unlikely. She's in Mallorca. I told Guy only yesterday."

"Why?"

Diana frowned at the phone, wondering why on earth she should have to answer to her crooked sister's son. "Because he's there …"

"Where?"

"In Mallorca. Now what's all this about?"

"I don't know where she is" he blurted, "I really don't know, Aunt Diana. I've also spoken to Aunt Pat. I know you're both furious and want Mum to burn in hell, and probably me too, but she really has disappeared!"

Danny knew he was skating on very thin ice appealing to either of his mother's sisters, but he was desperate to find her. Diana proved just as thorny as Pat. He tried playing the victim, telling her he had not benefitted financially either and wanted to put it right for everyone, but that his mother had duped him as well.

Diana delayed responding, thinking things were now heading in a very strange direction. Briefly, she wondered how much Danny really knew of Alison's treachery.

"Also," continued Danny, his voice pleading "there's been an accident." For a while the line fell silent.

"Yes, I know." Diana decided there was little to be gained by pretending otherwise. A sudden bleep on his mobile phone – he'd called Diana from his office landline – distracted him. He glanced at his mobile. A missed call from Justyn, then a text: *Better get here quick. Police think Grant was murdered!*

Danny refrained from sharing this information with Diana and ended their stilted conversation, as politely and quickly as he could.

★★★★★

Hours later Diana was to receive a bombshell of her own. Her niece, Clare, phoned to tell her that her son, Guy, was now helping the police with their enquiries in Mallorca. It took a moment for the news to sink in. As far as she knew Guy was with his cycling team. Had there been an accident? What could possibly have happened? She pressed Clare for more details but she didn't seem to know anything beyond the fact that Guy was in some kind of trouble.

Although in her eighties, Diana, remained relatively sprightly and agile but life had taken its toll; her skin had acquired a dull grey texture, her sunken brown eyes revealed an unfulfilled outlook on life. Recently she'd started to dwell on what had gone wrong. Sitting by the bay window of her semi-detached house in Hounslow, she watched morning shoppers rushing home to escape the rain. She knew it wouldn't be long before she went to the fridge to open her first bottle of Sauvignon for the day. Why was she rotting here alone while her sister, Alison was living in luxury in Mallorca? She looked at the pictures of Guy, adorning the mantelpiece and most of her sitting room wall: Guy passing out as an SAS officer, Guy in full military uniform on the day he left for Afghanistan, Guy, smiling, playing in the garden as a child with their puppy. She ached for him to ring. She knew she should never have married Donald, Guy's father. It had never been a happy marriage with 'the cold fish' – as her sister, Pat, had labelled him. She'd been happy working as a nurse but Donald insisted she quit when they married; later she'd helped out at the local surgery but was devastated when her boss said it was better for all concerned that she stood down. "You upset too many people Diana, you start too many fires. You're just too negative." Now, with too much time to think about things she found herself increasingly thinking of death, but it was the nothingness of her life that scared her most. She had resolved to do something about it, to get justice from her father's will; money would, at least, give her that opportunity. It was outrageous the way she and Pat had been excluded. She would go and find Alison and she would rescue Guy from whatever was going on with the police. The poor boy had suffered enough in his life. She resolved to fly to Mallorca as soon as possible.

"Justice will be done," she hollered at the world in general. But no one was listening. Calming down she phoned Pat.

Pat, younger and shorter than Diana, was returning to her cottage from the local church she attended in a village near Bury St. Edmunds. She heard her phone ringing as she walked in the front door. The line went dead as she lifted the receiver. She dialled 1471 and realised she'd missed a call from Diana. She was in no hurry to return it, fearing it would be another rant about their missing sister, Alison. She reflected that *her* life had been much steadier, much happier. Although widowed when Horace and Clare were so young, she'd enjoyed her career as an art historian. But in the end her good nature got the better of her and she called Diana back.

"We need to find Alison and get justice. We need to find Don Davenport too. I'm sure he brainwashed her."

"Well someone brainwashed father." Pat rejoined.

"Did they? I'm not so sure, he never liked us."

Pat ignored the remark. She knew Diana had endured a turbulent relationship with their father, but *she* hadn't. She didn't think this was the time or place to set the record straight. Diana, being the oldest had been closest to their mother, and when she died when Diana was only twelve she found it hard to accept the many nannies that Ken Stone hired to look after his daughters. It was as if, in some irrational way, Diana blamed her father for the early death of her beloved mother.

"And have you heard they've arrested Guy?" Pat didn't respond.

"The poor boy's had such a tough time. It was so hard for him when Donald walked out. He's been a war hero for goodness' sake – he should be given a medal."

The line fell silent; Pat's take on her sister's son was very different. She considered him strange, dangerous, possibly a bit unhinged. She never knew anyone whose mood could switch so fast. After another pause she quickly said,

"I'll join you in Mallorca. I'll sort out some accommodation and book the flights. Leave it to me."

*****

The police inspector was a big man with a paunch, beneath which, his trousers struggled to stay up. He summoned Justyn to his side office with a cursory wave of his hand. Looking belligerent, he told Justyn that he was free to leave.

Justyn nodded and quickly looked away to hide his relieved expression. He considered asking why but thought better of it. He just wanted to get out of there as soon as possible. He walked out as purposefully as he could, given that his hip was playing up. He was determined not to limp but he had to admit that he was feeling his age. It had been a humiliating and frightening experience and he was beginning to regret ever coming to Mallorca. He needed a shower and a stiff drink. Grant was dead, although he could hardly believe it, he'd had to identify his body and he'd ended up in a police cell. He decided to head back to the hotel to think about whether to stay or to just pack up and go home.

After a shower and a change of clothes Justyn began to shake off the shock of what had happened to him. He had come out to help Grant and felt duty-bound to stay and find out what was really going on. Perhaps he should contact Guy Roope, as he was on the island and may have some idea of what was happening. Although they hadn't met for years he still had a number for him and decided to give it a try.

The prospect of seeing Roope again after almost fifteen years filled Justyn with dread. The last time they had met was at Aunt Diana's seventieth birthday. Clare had begged him to go. It was at Diana's dowdy house somewhere near the A4. They'd had to park miles away as there was no off-road parking outside her house and they'd nearly got run over trying to cross the dual carriageway. Justyn remembered Guy sitting alone, not really interested in taking part. He was thickset with incredibly short hair and was wearing a singlet which showed off his huge muscles. Clare said she thought he looked like a skinhead. He was such an incongruous figure that all the guests avoided him and Justyn didn't remember having anything to do with him either.

He dialled and was surprised when he got an answer. He had assumed the number would have changed after so long. In the end the conversation was perfunctory; Guy was obviously not one for effusive conversations. They agreed to meet in Palma the following day at Justyn's favourite café in the market near the cathedral.

*****

Although now a lot older, Guy was still the kind of tough-looking figure you would not want to mess with.

"So, where's Aunty Alison?" He plonked himself down opposite Justyn and placed his heavy hands on the table in front of him.

"Clearly not where we thought!" Justyn stuck out a hand to greet him. Roope ignored it. "But you know what's the strangest thing? Danny's been completely wrong-footed by his own mother!"

Roope stared ahead. Justyn felt relieved when his mobile bleeped. It was a welcome distraction and was a text from Danny saying that he had just landed. Sensing Roope's impatience Justyn quickly typed in his reply: *Get a taxi to Palma. I'm in the Café de Palma, near the cathedral. Text me when you arrive.*

Horace had also texted Justyn telling him that he was now on the island. Reluctantly, he decided to text back, telling him where they would be. Fretting, he tapped his forefinger on the table awaiting Danny and Horace's arrival, willing Clare to join them. He had waited all morning for a call from her. He thought she should be there, helping him out. Roope was *her* cousin after all.

The two men sat at the table staring at one another and struggling to think of something to say. Justyn knew that Roope despised him and that any attempt at smalltalk would probably rile him. He suspected that Guy thought he was stuck up, scruffy and dissolute. Perhaps he was right. Justyn suggested they have something to eat and called the waiter over. Guy looked blankly at the menu so Justyn suggested they order two portions of jamon serrano and some bread, as he knew it would come quickly and would give them something to do while they waited for Danny. It worked. The time seemed to speed up and soon after they finished, Justyn felt two hands on the back of his shoulders. He swung round to see his old friend Danny. He had never been so pleased to see him. As always, Danny was dressed immaculately in a pale blue polo shirt, cream chinos and brown moccasins. He had changed very little over the years. He had remained slim and apart from some traces of grey in his ginger hair, he really hadn't aged at all. He made Justyn feel old and seedy.

Guy looked on doubtfully as the pair embraced, not quite sure what was going on or whether he liked it. Did Danny really not know what had happened? He wasn't willing to give him the benefit of the doubt. He nodded an acknowledgement. He'd always considered him a bit of a drip.

"What the hell happened to Grant?" Danny sounded shrill. His white skin was even paler than usual in the bright morning sun.

"God only knows!" Guy got going, "I suspect it really was an accident as we – my cycling group – apparently passed his hired car on the mountain road near Deià, and I can completely understand how it could happen there. But what do you *really* think's going on?"

"Who knows? I really don't. I thought Grant was stirring it, thought he was on another crusade that would only cause more trouble, like he was about the events in Cornwall all those years ago, but I was wrong. I'm really thrown by this. I mean, I'm in the dark as much as you guys. I know you all think Mum really screwed everyone over but somehow it doesn't make sense. Don Davenport *must* be with her. All that crap about a gentleman friend who was looking after her."

Danny looked down at the table. Guy slowly raised his hand and pointed an accusing finger at him.

"Does anyone know what happened to Davenport? I mean did anyone ever ask about him?"

Danny ignored him. His attention had been caught by some movement on the far side of the café. The others followed his gaze.

"I can't believe it, but look at that guy over there, the one just leaving. He looks just like Don Davenport." Danny sprang to his feet to get a better look.

"Seems unlikely, but you may be right." Justyn was craning his neck to get a better view. The person they'd spotted moved away hurriedly, elbowing his way through the throngs of tourists.

"They must be here …" Justyn had tried to ease the tension between Danny and Guy, but Danny didn't hear. He was already on his feet, scuttling past crowded tables of people sitting out in the midday sun and nearly tripping over a waiter carrying a full tray of drinks. Justyn and Guy tried to follow but Danny moved too quickly and soon vanished.

Justyn ordered two more coffees and settled back down in the chair next to Roope. A warm breeze ruffled the palm trees behind them. He couldn't believe he was going to have to spend yet more time with this man. But he decided the best thing would be to get Roope to relax so began by asking him about the SAS. Roope stared at his hands, answering in monosyllables. He clearly didn't want to talk about it. Justyn tried a different tack.

"So what do you think of me?"

"What do I think of you?" Roope, repeated the question. Justyn nodded.

"Well your hair's too long for a start, certainly for your age. You used to be in some rock band or other, didn't you? Did you do drugs?" Justyn raised an eyebrow, ready to fire back, when he caught sight of Horace, walking heavily towards them.

"What the? … oh hooray, it's Horace!"

Horace's 'hail fellow well met' style grated on both of them, but the three knew they had more to gain by getting on with each other than not.

"So where's the bitch?" Horace launched in.

Justyn rolled his eyes and gave Horace a quick resumé of what had been happening. Guy appeared distracted, looking around, unimpressed by Justyn's account and Horace seemed more interested in scrutinizing Guy. Here was the cousin he'd grown up with, there being only a year between them. He had always considered him a bit strange, even obsessive; he imagined him even now having bicycle clips attached to his trousers under the table. He also knew he had been in the SAS and couldn't fathom how that had happened. Guy was one of those people – a complete anathema to Horace – who worked out for hours every day. However, not for a second did he think Guy's group could be responsible for Grant Morrison's fatal accident.

"Anyway, just before you arrived we were sure we saw Don Davenport, just over there," Justyn pointed to the exit of the restaurant, where customers were queuing to pay their bills. Horace looked aghast.

"What? Why the deuce didn't you stop him?"

"Danny tried."

"And … ?"

"He just disappeared. We're sure your Aunt Alison's on the island and pretty sure she's with Don Davenport. But they're not where we all thought. Grant's dead. No one believes it was an accident. There's some serious shit going down. Guy and I have both been taken in for questioning!" He shot a glance at Guy as he spoke.

"Well, don't look at me!" Guy sounded wounded, but Justyn continued.

"I know you and your team had nothing to do with it." Guy half smiled, reassured, but still bristling at the idea of his cycling team being implicated.

"Well, whatever the hell happened to Grant Morrison, my sister's very upset about it, thinks it a very rum state of affairs, very rum indeed!" Horace spoke as if he were addressing a political rally.

"She should do." Justyn considered whether he should fill the two cousins in on all the facts from the past; the fatalities in Cornwall in the 1970s and the recent suicide of Suzie Hughes-Webb. He wasn't sure how much they knew but, after reflection, decided to give a potted history. He revealed details of Grant's investigations back in Cornwall and how he was spooked by a child's voice singing "Half a Pound of Tuppenny Rice" in the dead of night in Zennor. Looking first at Guy, then at Horace, he felt that something in their reaction suggested the story was not in any way unfamiliar to either of them.

★★★★★

Danny Galvin watched the man with the bald head walk out of a leather accessories shop in Valldemossa, having successfully tracked him all the way from Palma. Unbeknown to him, so had someone else. The man he presumed to be Don Davenport, crossed the road and took a seat at a pavement café. Danny put on his sunglasses, pulled down his baseball cap and watched Davenport run a finger down the menu.

He texted Justyn: *Quick JS get to Valldemossa. Bar Tramuntana. He's here. Hasn't spotted me yet. Need your help. He doesn't know you so won't suspect.*

Justyn read the text and plonked a fifty euro note on the table. He got up, gave the others a quick nod, and left without saying a word. Guy Roope and Horace Loosemore looked bemused, fidgeting in their seats, unnerved by Justyn's sudden exit and both wanting to escape from the other.

Guy had never warmed to Horace. He thought he was inauthentic, always pretending to be a pompous, eccentric Englishman but in reality he was just a bore and a bluffer.

★★★★★

Justyn decided to indulge himself and hire a Harley-Davidson. He'd noticed a hire shop nearby. He could hardly believe that it was possible to rent such a thing but he couldn't think of a faster or more fun way of getting to Valldemossa. Even though he was now a fairly successful designer, at heart he was still an old rocker, with hair that he'd just been told was too long. To hell with arthritic hips. The man in the hire shop looked sceptical and charged what Justyn thought was an over-inflated price for the deposit. When he added the cost of hiring a jacket and a helmet, the bill was extortionate. But soon Justyn was exhilarated by the instant speed and couldn't help smiling as he roared across the plains towards Valldemossa. In only thirty minutes he'd arrived at the beautiful, medieval town.

He spotted Danny at the café. He had managed to find a corner table where he could see Davenport but couldn't be seen by him. Justyn was surprised to be neither greeted nor even acknowledged by Danny as he was sure he had seen him.

Then Justyn realised why. Sitting only a few feet away, at the next table but one, was none other than Don Davenport. It was definitely him. Justyn stopped in his tracks but quickly got the measure of the situation, understanding why Danny was unable to move. The slightest thing could give him away. A couple of times Davenport looked round at the people sitting near him. Danny was partly hidden by the 'Mallorcan Daily Bulletin', and just nodded when the waiter asked if he wanted another espresso.

Justyn sauntered towards a vacant table, fighting off a very uncharacteristic urge; he suddenly wanted to punch Davenport, to hit him so hard he would fall to the ground. The thought did not linger, he had no intention of ever returning to police custody on this island again. Violence could wait. Before Justyn could place an order, Davenport was on his feet shuffling awkwardly towards the counter. By good fortune, Davenport walked towards the same car park that Justyn had used for his Harley. Danny followed them both at a discreet distance.

As they entered the car park, Davenport unlocked his car – an Audi R8 – as he walked towards it. Out of nowhere, from behind, a hooded stranger grabbed Davenport in an arm lock and forced him to the ground. Startled, Justyn bellowed "Oi!." The attacker ran off just as quickly as he had appeared.

Justyn and Danny raced after the assailant who vaulted a fence and disappeared; then they heard the sudden revving of an engine that they presumed was a getaway car. They turned back to see Davenport hurriedly reversing out of his parking space. Seconds later, back on his motorbike, Justyn was following Davenport on the road to Deià.

★★★★★

The throaty roar of the motorbike alerted Davenport to the fact that he was being followed. Justyn had to concentrate hard. The Audi was trying to speed away and when a coach pulled out in front of Justyn, he had to slow down. It wasn't safe to overtake on the high, twisting roads and there was too much traffic coming the other way. He managed to keep Davenport's car in sight, and watched it indicate right as the coach in front slowed down and also turned right. Suddenly, without warning, the car pulled across the oncoming traffic and turned left. Justyn followed, narrowly missing a taxi. The track was so rough that Justyn had to slow down or risk being thrown off his bike. Just as he did, an ancient tractor pulled out in front of him. The track was so narrow that he couldn't overtake, even on a motorbike. He had to watch the Audi disappear into the distance while the tractor belched clouds of diesel fumes at him. He feared he had lost Davenport. He drove past secluded villas, carob trees and oleander bushes until eventually the tractor turned off and headed for a remote finca on the horizon and Justyn was at last able to drive unimpeded down to the end of the road.

Eventually he reached the car park by the beach. The Audi was nowhere to be seen. Frustrated, Justyn turned and drove back up the winding hill to the junction of the Deià to Sóller road. Miraculously, Danny's Ford came into view and like a Grand Prix steward, Justyn waved his arms at his friend to stop.

He ran up to Danny's car, relieved to have an ally in this crazy chase.

"He's down there somewhere. Don't ask me where. Must be in one of the villas. They're all private. Mostly protected by automatic gates. I went all the way to the bottom and it's a dead end – no sign of his Audi." Danny smiled warmly at his friend, grateful for his support. He was quiet for a while.

"Don't worry, I'll hang around here and check things out, and thanks." Justyn clapped his friend firmly on the shoulder.

"No problem, I'm heading back to the hotel. I've got a few things I must do. Good luck!" Justyn felt no need to hang around and revved up the motorbike to get away quickly.

★★★★★

It wasn't long before Justyn was making his way down the corridor towards his room, taking off his leather motorcycle jacket as he walked. As he turned the key in the lock he heard a noise from inside the room. As he went in he checked right then left and couldn't see anyone, so he cautiously entered the bathroom. Then he saw her, standing in front of the mirror, her reflected smile beaming at him. Clare Loosemore.

"Well, who's a dark horse, then?" He was unsure whether to move closer and embrace her or wait for her to respond. Her warm, affectionate look in the mirror suggested she would be responsive. She didn't speak and just carried on smiling in a sort of triumphant but slightly uncertain way. He was struck by her large, brown, puppy-like eyes. He had forgotten how stunning they were. She still had the ability to melt his heart with her smile. She half turned and Justyn realised just how much he had missed her, how the six month separation had been such a waste of time. When she turned back to the mirror, still smiling, Justyn wrapped his arms around her waist, half expecting, almost dreading, he would be pushed away. To his delight she moved her arms to try to wrap them behind his back, failing but stroking his sides gently in the process. She turned and fell into his arms.

"I've missed you so much!" Justyn almost whispered, tenderly kissing her neck and running his fingers over the top of her shoulders. Swept up by increasing excitement he stepped back and hurriedly placed the "Do Not Disturb" sign outside the door. It was not the right moment for his phone to ring.

"I've seen it!" Danny sounded euphoric.

"What?"

"The villa where Mum and Davenport are holed up – I followed the police car to their door. They didn't see me."

"But did you see Davenport?"

"No, but the police seem very interested in whoever lives there."

"Where are you, Danny?" Justyn barked, irritated. He was more focused on Clare slipping out of a blue cotton dress, revealing nothing underneath. Her eyes were fixed on his.

"I'm hiding out of view, shielded by a large rock and a police car's blocking the entrance to the drive. They haven't seen me so I think I'll hang out here for a while." Danny's voice sounded calm, but barely audible, as if he was commentating on a golf tournament from the edge of the fairway. "Oh, by the way, Horace and Guy are on the way to your hotel. Hope you don't mind. I gave them the address."

"Oh no! Look, Danny, keep me posted, I'm a little bit busy at the moment."

"Yeah, sure;" Danny watched the two *policías* return to their car, and speed away. Guessing the large wooden gates were about to shut, he dashed through them into the front garden. The garage door was open but he was surprised to see the parked Audi was not the one driven by Don Davenport. He knew his cars and this Audi A4 TDI was different to the car he had seen hurrying out of the car park at Valldemossa. He cursed. At one point he had hidden behind a rock for a pee and remembered hearing a car speeding away. It must have been Davenport. Assuming his mother was secreted somewhere in the villa, he stopped thinking of himself as an intruder and made his way up a narrow winding path to the front door. With a rising sense of indignation, he felt he had every right to be welcomed by his own mother. Then through a window he saw the silhouette of a man standing with his back to him. The man turned round and nothing in Danny's life had prepared him for what would come next.

★★★★★

"Dad!" Danny grabbed the handrail at the top of the stone path for support. All this time he had been preparing to meet his mother. Never, in his wildest dreams, did he think he would ever see his father again. How could he? He had been dead for over twenty years. Danny had been told about his death while he was away in Mykonos. But there was no doubt that the man in front of him, his face now more lined and angular, was none other than his own father. He took a step forward, Danny took a step back, half-wondering if he was looking at a ghost. Surely this was a cruel and extraordinary trick.

How *could* this man be his father?

He tensed as his father reached towards him. Danny felt his head starting to spin. He grabbed the rail again for support, but the dizziness got worse and he lurched forward into his father's arms.

When Danny came round he heard a muffled voice asking, "Can you hear me Danny?" His eyes widened as he saw the ambulance outside. Two paramedics were with him, one unfolding a stretcher. He had no recollection of what happened next, as he passed out again and when he came to he was in the ambulance stretched out on a bed. Opposite him, on a small seat, sat one of the paramedics. He kept talking to him presumably in an attempt to stop him passing out again.

"Como te llamas? Como te sientes?"

Danny looked blank.

"How you feel?"

"Okay, Okay thanks, but what's happening?"

"You faint, we are taking you to hospital. No te preocupes. You have tests."

Danny felt the ambulance man's hand on his shoulder, as if to restrain him.

"You like futbol? Manchester United?"

Danny knew he could bore for Britain on this subject but was in no mood for small talk, he had just seen his father, the man he thought had died more than twenty years ago. How could he talk about anything else? Slowly he muttered "My father." The paramedic raised his right eyebrow. Danny offered no more, the paramedic became fretful.

"Tu padre?"

Danny thought nothing could be more surreal. Here he was listening to crazy Spanglish when he had just suffered the most traumatic event of his whole life.

"I've just seen my father." Danny released the words slowly, carefully; words he thought he would never say again. At the same time he was struggling to find any words from his long forgotten schoolboy Spanish to try to explain what was going on.

"Es un problema?"

"Si"

"Por que?"

"Because he died a long time ago." He racked his brains for the Spanish word for dead. "Muerto."

Danny's voice trailed off, he lifted up his head, leant forward and vomited all over the bed.

★★★★★

Lying on what seemed to be a bed on a trolley, Danny had time to reflect on his life. He had grown up in awe of his father.

But as a teenager, he couldn't help feeling that his father was disappointed in him; that he was inadequate in some way. He thought back to that day, that very awkward day, when he had told his parents he was gay. The infamous 'coming out of the closet' family discussion had not gone well; apart from Sharon, his sister, who leapt out of her seat and hugged him, exclaiming, "I'm so proud of you!" He knew she'd known for years.

He recalled that late July Sunday afternoon with the sun casting long shadows over the manicured back lawn of the family home in Chelmsford, the peace of the setting at odds with the impending storm that he knew would break when he confronted his parents with the truth. He had never told them the real reason for the break-up of his engagement to Suzie Hughes-Webb. He'd announced he was going to Mykonos to live with Julian. His father thought it was nothing more than one of his pranks. Ironically, their relationship had improved as his father's fortunes declined. First, he lost his job as an accountant, then things went from bad to worse when he got involved with a building project in Penzance. The development failed and he lost most of his money. He sank into a long depression and withdrew from the world. Fortunately, he had kept a little capital back from that project, and Danny had been grateful when he invested it in his car dealership. As it grew, his father took vicarious pride in his success. He even suspected his father had grown proud of him.

As he drifted in and out of consciousness, waiting for an ECG, he tried to make sense of what had happened. So many times over the past twenty years he had held imaginary conversations with his father. Often it would be as simple as telling him where Spurs had finished the season. Other times he would ask him for advice about the business. Sometimes it featured news of his partner, Oliver, or more specifically, difficulties with their relationship. His father had long since come to terms with his sexuality; the problem was he knew he'd never come to like Oliver. Danny grew agitated thinking of all those conversations that he had never had. How could his father have treated him so cruelly? Then he grew calmer, thinking it may just be a weird dream. At that moment he glimpsed, through a pane of smoked glass, his friend Justyn arriving in Reception. He could just about hear him talking to the receptionist,

"I must see him. He's my best friend and he's going to need help."

"So, you're not his next of kin and you're not involved in a relationship?" She was working through her checklist in impeccable English.

"Look, I know you have procedures but please, this man, er, friend, Danny Galvin, doesn't have any next of kin, at least not as far as we can discover on the island."

On hearing this Danny was tempted to shout out – so flimsy was the dividing glass between them – but the strength to do so eluded him. He heard Justyn agree to wait in reception, after he was told that he would be allowed to drive Danny home, as long as all the tests were normal.

Danny relaxed a little but a few minutes later he couldn't help overhearing the receptionist again. This time she was talking on the phone:

"And you are who again? Your name is Peter Beal, and you say you're Danny's father!"

Justyn was also listening to the conversation.

"So now you say you are Paul Galvin, and you are Danny's father!" She raised her eyebrows. Was this man a time-waster? For some reason that Justyn couldn't fathom, she suddenly chose to believe him.

Danny couldn't resist smiling. His father had taken the name of one of their favourite Spurs players from the 1970s, Phil Beale, changing the Christian name from Phil to Peter to avoid others recognising it. He must have suspected that one day Danny would find him and work out the connection.

CHAPTER FOUR

"They're coming to join us." Clare announced, feeling a flutter of apprehension.

"Who?"

"Mum and Aunt Pat."

Justyn's face hardened, "They're a bit old for this sort of caper, aren't they?" He was concerned that Clare's mother, Pat Loosemore, would complicate matters unnecessarily for both her daughter and her son, Horace. He had always got on well with Pat as she was the most normal of the sisters. Diana Roope, on the other hand, the older sister and Guy's mother, was an unknown quantity, but he did know that Guy's family life had been dysfunctional and unhappy. More frustratingly, Danny hadn't been released from hospital after his ECG, and was being kept in overnight for an MRI brain scan the following day.

"They'll be in Pollença," Clare turned away, "Some friends of Mum's have a lovely villa there, it's not far but they won't be on top of us." She looked back over her shoulder, giving a flirtatious smile. "By the way, I'm meeting up with an old friend later. Her name's Leia. I met her a while back when I was doing some PR for the Chopin festival."

"Oh really?"

"Yes. She's amazing. She's in her twenties and all by herself. An orphan really. She works part time in a supermarket, part time in a hotel and helps with the Chopin Festival. When I met her she was helping someone with their research on Chopin's piano."

Justyn was only half listening. He had something he wanted to tell Clare and he was wondering how best to say it.

"I just wonder if the book ever got finished." Clare knew she was prattling but wanted to share her news, even though she knew Justyn wasn't that interested.

"What book?" said Justyn

"The one on Chopin's piano!"

"Oh. Right."

"Anyway she's met a new man and wants to talk about him. He's English and much older than her. Can't wait to hear all about it."

"Mmm. Clare?"

"Yes."

" I need to tell you something really important."

"Yeah?" Clare's eyes were still smiling. At that moment she thought nothing could go wrong in her world.

"Er ... this is really weird, Clarezy."

"What?"

"Well yesterday at the hospital, I heard – you're really not going to believe this – that Danny's father," he hesitated a moment, "is still alive!"

"Alive? Danny's Dad alive? What on earth are you talking about?"

"He's not only alive, but he's here, Clarezy, in Mallorca."

Clare fell back into a chair. She knew Justyn well enough to know that he wouldn't make up a story like that.

"But he died, what was it, twenty years ago?"

"Allegedly."

"Allegedly ... Everyone knew ..."

"Did you go the funeral?"

"No, but I'm sure most of the family did."

"Did they? Who did? When did they go? Where was it?" Justyn now wondered if there had been a funeral at all. Suddenly the spectre of the travelling Aunts took on some appeal. Perhaps they could help after all.

"But it just doesn't make any sense, JS. Even if he is alive, why would he be here, on Mallorca, when his wife and her lover came here, taking everyone's inheritance with them?" A look of concern on Clare's face told him "please don't ruin everything now with this ridiculous nonsense!"

"Look, I know this seems highly, incredibly unlikely, but please believe me. I know there are far too many unanswerable questions at the moment, but I really did hear Paul Galvin ask after his son at the hospital yesterday. It was completely freaky and quite embarrassing."

"Why?"

"Well, I'd just tried to bullshit my way into seeing Danny. I told them I was his closest friend and that he had no family!"

Clare half-smiled, moving over to sit beside Justyn on the bed. She was beginning to believe him but coming to terms with this very unexpected and unlikely news was proving difficult. She kissed him gently on the cheek. At least the shock hadn't diminished the attraction she felt for him. In fact, if anything she found his new assertiveness rather sexy. Nothing, she resolved, would get in the way of their future now. Not even a re-incarnated person from twenty years ago. Clare flicked a strand of white hair away from Justyn's right eye, looking at him quizzically.

"Why did you come here?"

"You mean why did I come here to Mallorca?" Clare nodded. "Well, ever since we agreed to that six month split – moratorium on the relationship –" Justyn mimicked the counsellor, "I've wanted you. Wanted you more than ever, Clare Loosemore." He saw her lips open as if she was about to speak and then shut again before she said anything. It was a very endearing habit of hers. He never knew whether it was just an unconscious tic or whether she genuinely had something to say and then would think better of it. Either way it added to the unknowable part of her which both fascinated and beguiled him.

"I've often thought if I could help your family in any way to get some redress on your grandfather's will, then I would maybe have done something a bit heroic!" Justyn laughed, feeling foolish. Clare beamed back and as she got to her feet, he put up a hand to stop her. "And there's another story you should know from a long time ago ..." Clare sat down again. Justyn continued. "It concerns Hector Wallace."

"Who?"

"Hector 'The Office' Wallace!" This time Clare didn't do her delayed speech routine but tapped his knee affectionately.

"Tell me about him."

"In the early seventies my family used to spend our summer holidays in West Cornwall. I've bored you about it enough, I know, but there was this eccentric character who stayed in the hotel, called Hector Wallace. He went with his elderly aunt in the same two weeks in August as the rest of us; he dressed in a checked suit, wore a monocle and used to take the long walk down the hotel drive at midday, and every night after dinner to the local pub, 'The Cornish Arms' which he re-christened 'The Office'. I sometimes joined him, usually when I gate-crashed the pub band. But I really got to know Hector late at night as we sat together drinking. After we were slung out of the pub, we'd head back to the hotel; we'd both annoy and amuse the night porters. He was almost old enough to be my dad but I liked him. We were kindred spirits. We were both kind of eccentric and saw ourselves as outsiders."

"And?"

"Well, one night Hector told me his life story, how he was abused from about the age of thirteen onwards. It was one of the most distressing stories I'd ever heard. He was such a gentle, kind man."

"But who the hell abused him?" Clare interrupted, watching Justyn pace around the room.

"Well, this is where the story gets really difficult. You see Clare," he hesitated, "it was Ken Stone. Your grandfather." He turned to face her.

"What!" Clare jumped to her feet. He moved to soothe her, placing an arm around her shoulders. She pushed it away.

"I'm so sorry, I know this is a terrible shock; I'm not telling you to hurt you, but I think you should know what happened."

"Why? How are you so sure, Justyn? Are you after justice for your friend Hector Wallace, after all these years?" The blood rushed to her face.

"No, no point," he paused, trying to calm her with a wave of his hand, as if he was directing traffic to slow down, "he was found drowned a few days after he told me his story. Washed up naked on Carbis Bay Beach."

"So what are you saying, JS, is that Grandpa murdered your Hector Wallace?" The sparkle had gone from her eyes. She looked deflated. Justyn sat down on the bed.

"No, but –"

"But what?"

"There is something else you should know from that time …" She felt her heart skip a beat.

"You mean there's more?"

"There were relations of yours who used to stay at the hotel at the same time as us."

"Who?"

"The Galvins." Clare felt nauseous and protested that she'd heard all this before. Justyn, supporting her, gently eased her back next to him on the bed.

"I'm sorry, Clarezy, I really am, I know there's enough baggage with your family's past, but I really wanted to do something positive for you."

"And how do you think coming to Mallorca achieves that? By finding Aunt Alison and telling her that her father ruined someone called Hector Wallace's life over forty years ago, that her father was a child molester. I don't see how that really helps, Justyn."

"Not on its own, no, you're right. But there's something else." The last words sounded like an afterthought and hung in the air. "Can you really cope with any more?" Clare nodded, hiding her real feelings.

"There was someone else, who is now also very relevant to all that's happened, who was in Cornwall all those years ago."

"Who?"

"Don Davenport. He never stayed at our hotel, he based his family somewhere nearby. Well, to cut a long story short, he was spotted in an amorous situation with your Aunt Alison."

"Where?"

"In St Ives."

"Okay, as a matter of fact, I seem to recall you've actually told me all this before." Sighing, irritated, she added, "But who spotted them anyway?"

"I did."

"I'm trying to figure out where you're going with this JS, are you possibly, in any way, suggesting that Don Davenport might have had Hector Wallace murdered all those years ago?" Justyn looked away, Clare heard him mutter.

"Very possibly."

She shot him a frightened glance.

"You see there was a cine-film, that only came to light last year, and it showed Hector being lured on to the beach when he was drunk. Later that night, he drowned. Paul Galvin features in that particular film talking to the man who enticed Hector towards the sea. I need to see the film again. I have a very strong feeling I might recognise someone else in it now. I need to see Danny's copy."

*****

Danny was sitting with his legs crossed opposite the neurologist in the small consulting room in the hospital. He looked and felt drained and wasn't particularly interested in the diagnosis being given by the slim, severe looking consultant. He was sure there was nothing wrong with him. He had merely fainted from the shock of seeing his father again.

"So I fainted, what's new? It often happens."

The consultant was undeterred and continued with the diagnosis.

"We've discovered a small neo-enteric cyst on the base of your brain. We think it's an incidental and shouldn't cause you further problems. We suggest you have it checked in a year's time, just to keep an eye on it." The consultant was taken aback by Danny's indifference; he appeared not even to be listening.

"So, you're free to go, which you appear very keen to do, but make sure you rest up today, and probably tomorrow as well." Danny didn't react but continued to stare ahead of him; he knew why he'd had the MRI scan, the heart monitoring had triggered it, but that was as unimportant to him right now, as the cyst he had just been told about. What he couldn't understand was the vision of his father at the villa, which kept coming back into his head. That his father had then called the hospital boosted him massively. But where was he now? Danny slowly lifted himself from his seat, thanked the specialist, shook his hand, and stepped into the corridor. He rang Justyn and paced up and down while he waited for an answer.

"Hi, can you please rescue me? You know where."

"Sure, give me forty minutes."

★★★★★

Justyn turned to look at Clare who was lying peacefully asleep. Kissing her gently on the forehead, he climbed out of bed.

"Where're you going?" The quietness of her voice couldn't conceal its tension.

"Just to collect Danny. Do you mind if I take your car?" He didn't wait for her reply. He felt there was no point telling her anything else at this stage. He looked back from the doorway. She pulled a face at him, making a good show of pretending to be offended.

Danny was waiting outside the main entrance to the hospital and when Justyn arrived he barely waited for him to stop before he jumped into the car, throwing his head back as he landed in the seat.

"I've got to find him JS. I've got to get back to my Dad. He asked for me at the hospital, you heard, he was on the phone. I've got to find him today!"

Justyn nodded.

"Are you sure you're fit and well enough to do anything today. What were you told?"

"Oh the usual, rest up, don't go out for a bit, but I'm fine! Look, I know why I passed out. Who wouldn't seeing their dead father alive. No, I'm fine. It won't happen again. Now I just need to find him again."

"But," Justyn hesitated, "are you sure it's him? I heard that a Peter Beal asked for you at the hospital. I mean can you be 100 percent sure?"

"Oh yes, I'm sure!"

Justyn groaned on hearing how the alias was concocted.

"Yes, I'm sure, it's him. It's definitely him. He's alive and well."

"Okay" Justyn turned to look at his friend, easing his foot on the accelerator pedal, "So what can I do to help?"

"After I've freshened up, can you drop me at the top of the road where we stopped yesterday, just outside Deià on the route to Sóller?" Justyn nodded.

"By the way, I know it's a totally unrelated subject, but do you still have that cine-film taken in the pub that last night in Cornwall back in '72?"

"I haven't got it here but the film's on my laptop if you want to see it."

"Well one good turn deserves another. I'd like to borrow it."

"Sure," Danny answered, distracted,

"Thanks." Justyn breathed a slow sigh of relief.

The more Justyn thought about it, the more angry he became. He sort of understood why Danny wanted to reconnect with his father, but on the other hand, he had behaved so badly that he also wouldn't have been surprised if he'd never wanted to see him again. What kind of father behaves the way Paul Galvin had?

Driving fast, he became more and more anxious. What if Clare took fright and left him again? It was all getting out of control. He dreaded the elderly sisters arriving and then searching for Alison Galvin and Don Davenport when there were so many other things to worry about. Who was the hooded figure who attacked the person they believed to be Don Davenport in Valldemossa? Where did Davenport go if not to the villa where Danny found Paul Galvin? He felt he couldn't share his concerns with Danny as he was on a mission of his own. They travelled in silence, both consumed with apprehension at what the next few days might bring. At the same time Justyn couldn't help suppressing a smile at the thought of he and Danny, two middle-aged men, behaving like Starsky and Hutch. He decided not to share that thought either, as Danny seemed in no mood for jokes.

When they reached the hotel they wandered over to the pool and slumped into reclining seats, two dishevelled and incongruous figures, still locked in their private worlds. Danny soon struggled to his feet, saying, "I'm going to get changed. I'll be back in an hour."

Justyn waved to the waiter and ordered a gin and tonic. When it arrived, he quickly drained the glass. He thought of ringing Clare. As he stared at the holiday-makers enjoying the sun, he had a sudden urge to smash the glass on the nearby concrete path. This all suddenly seemed so pointless. None of them were any nearer to finding Alison Galvin and Don Davenport. He was staring at scattered fragments of a story, just as he imagined his shattered glass would look. He fell into a doze.

"Are you ready?" Danny interrupted his slumber.

"Are you sure you really want to do this?" Danny nodded. Justyn tried one last time to put him off: "You know what me and Grant used to call you – 'Desperate Dan'!" Danny grunted, more in amusement than anger. Justyn caught his look and saw his resolve.

Soon they were sitting in the car looking at the same wooden gates Danny had seen earlier.

"This is it."

"So, what's the plan? Hang around here for hours on end, hoping someone will turn up and open the gates?"

"Yes." Danny got out of the car saying, "If you don't hear from me by nightfall, call the police." Justyn stared at the huge gates, thinking this was a very bad plan. He started the engine, leaving Danny to dart around the pine and carob trees, trying to find a good hideout where he could avoid being seen by cars going up and down the narrow road to and from the rocky beach below.

★★★★★

The weather began to close in. It was humid and airless and Danny heard a faint rumble of thunder in the distance. He didn't really fancy sitting here in a storm.

Luckily he didn't have to wait long. A van arrived with MANTENIMIENTO DE PISCINAS written on the side. The driver opened the gates with a remote control, and slowly entered the stone driveway, stopping behind the garage. Danny, waiting just outside the gates, knew the sensors would soon close them. As they began to move he saw the man disappear around the side of the house carrying a large tool box and what looked like a vacuum cleaner. Quickly, Danny slipped into the garden and hid behind a tree while the gates closed. He then followed the man round the back. There was a huge kidney-shaped swimming pool, looking still and inviting in the searing heat. From a half hidden position Danny could see what the man was doing. He watched him unlock a door to the basement where he presumed the controls for the pool were housed. Danny waited until he came out again and while the man had his back turned to start cleaning the pool, Danny slipped through the door. The basement was huge. In one corner was the machinery for the pool but the rest was full of gym equipment: a treadmill, a rowing machine, an exercise bike and a cross-trainer. Danny spotted a large tiered rack of dumbbells out of view of the door and decided he could hide behind it. He could see a staircase next to the boiler which he confidently assumed would lead to an internal entrance to the villa.

He crouched low, checking his watch every five minutes, listening to rippling noises, as the water was treated. He had no idea how long the maintenance man would be but decided he would just stay put until he had finished. He had no desire to make his acquaintance.

With plenty of time to think, Danny anticipated his father's incredulity at discovering him in his villa. It was not a normal way to re-establish familial relations, but he would tell him how the hospital had refused to help him trace his father's call. His father might wonder why he hadn't rung the bell. He panicked at the thought. Even at his age he feared more rejection. Hadn't he been rejected for the last twenty years?

All the time he was hiding, he had assumed his father would appear to check the pool man's work so he was surprised to hear the man lock the door from the outside. He was now effectively locked in. He hoped he was right about the stairs he had spotted and that he would be able to get out that way. Danny wasted no time and raced up the stairs. There was a door at the top. He turned the handle. It moved, but the door didn't open. He tried again but the noise had apparently alerted a woman on the other side.

"Hang on I'll unlock the door. It's José, the pool man, interrupting us again."

Her voice alerted Paul Galvin and he shuffled down the corridor from the kitchen to see what was going on. Something told him it wasn't the maintenance man.

"Wait Monika, let me open the door." But he was too late.

Monika opened the door and gasped.

"Peter, there is strange man here!"

"It's alright, it's alright Monika, I know who he is. You'd better come in Danny, I've been expecting you!"

Danny fell into his father's arms. He didn't faint this time. He wept. Embarrassed little sobs graduating into wails.

"It's alright, it's alright." Paul comforted him as best he could, holding his son tight, feeling the weight of the lost twenty years. "Let's go through here and sit down." Danny struggled to speak. He was desperate not to break down. He cursed himself for being so pathetic. Paul sank into his chair as if he was about to watch a favourite TV programme.

"I tried to see you at the hospital. What's going on? But first, let's get you something. A drink? Tea?"

Paul was babbling, not knowing what to say and Danny couldn't really believe any of this was happening. Here he was with a father he thought was dead and he was offering him a cup of tea! On the other hand anything would have seemed strange in such a surreal meeting. There was a long silence. Both men struggling with complex and conflicting emotions.

"I don't know how to apologise, don't really know what to say at all, how to put the record straight. All I can say, Dan, is I never meant to hurt you or Sharon."

A loud crack of thunder interrupted him. Paul, leaning forward opposite his son, confessed in one long, disjointed monologue that Danny's mother and Davenport all knew that Ken Stone, Danny's grandfather, was a child abuser, and how they had taken the opportunity to blackmail him. Danny noticed his father's laboured breathing; his hands were shaking and he called out to Monika to bring his inhaler. Frowning, he grabbed it.

"Damn my asthma, it gets worse every day." Danny edged forward on the settee, looking alarmed. The wind rose in intensity, whistling through the room and filling the house and garden with foreboding.

"Dad, just tell me why you did this? How you could deny me and Sharon all these years?" Before he finished his sentence, Paul's breathing became forced.

"It was your mother's idea, hers and ..." He collapsed, falling forward. His head hit the floor and his eyes seemed to roll back into his head. Monika screamed. Danny shot forward, quickly easing his father onto his side and into the recovery position. Paul, momentarily stabilised, struggled to speak; Danny and Monika, leaning in, just caught his last words: "I love you." His eyes were fixed on his son and seemed to be searching for forgiveness. He took one last breath and was gone.

★★★★★

Danny's recollection of what happened next was to remain a blur for many years; he remembered telling Monika to call a doctor, who he thought arrived surprisingly swiftly. Monika fussed around, alternating between talking excitedly one moment and crying the next. The doctor, a thick-set Spanish man of middle years had been blunt: "Señor has suffered a heart attack, his pulse has stopped …"

Monika fell to the ground, moaning, "Oh my poor Peter, my love, my love," before quickly recovering her composure and suggesting they call an ambulance and a lawyer that she knew.

"No point calling an ambulance," the doctor remarked.

"And we don't need a lawyer, we need an undertaker." Danny surprised himself as he took control. He felt he was in a dream. None of the normal rules applied. He politely ushered the doctor out, thanking him for coming and was met with a resigned shrug. Turning back he had questions for Monika. For a start, who was she? For the first time he looked at her closely, guessing she was in her late twenties and from Eastern Europe. She was tall and glamorous with long blond hair and dark roots.

In less than an hour, the undertakers were lifting his father out of the house and taking him to his next destination: the very same mortuary where Grant had been taken just a few days earlier. The wind had fallen, the night was still and Danny went outside, looking up to a full moon.

A long and complicated chapter had ended in his life. "Rest in peace, Dad," he found himself saying out loud. It had been a reconciliation … of sorts.

CHAPTER FIVE

"Pollença, they're in Pollença!" Clare shouted out the news of her mother Pat's arrival.

Roope had heard the same from his mother, Diana. Justyn was wandering around by the bar unable to concentrate, distressed that he'd heard nothing from Danny. As if on cue his phone rang:

"Don't call the Guardia Civil. I'm Okay, but Dad's not. He's dead!"

"What, Danny? Are you sure? What's happened?"

"He's dead, Justyn, my old mate, he really is dead this time."

Justyn stared at the phone: "Are you Okay?" A fearful thought took him; "Danny how did he die? You haven't ... ?"

"Course not! No. Course I haven't done anything. It seems he's suffered a massive heart attack. Monika tells me he's been having TIAs lately. "

"Who's Monika?"

"His lady friend, been with him here for a while apparently."

"Do you want me to collect you?"

"Yes please. I've a few phone calls to make – Sharon, for a start. She knows nothing about any of this."

"Okay. Make the calls. By the way Clare says the aunts are in Pollença." Danny didn't respond. He'd become distracted by the sound of Monika on her phone, giving an account of everything that had happened. Who was she talking to? Her real lover? He knew his elderly father wasn't really her partner. Only an idiot would have believed that. Something about her worried him. She seemed to be acting out a role. He hoped she had been kind to his father, even though he wasn't sure he'd deserved it. Had she seen an old man off before? Did she stand to benefit financially? Was this the outcome she had been waiting for? He fixed his eyes on her. For the first time Danny wondered about his reincarnated father's legacy. Who would hold the Will? He resolved to find the lawyer Monika mentioned. There was no point interrogating her further now, the key to everything was his father's last words: "It was your mother's idea, hers and …"

Now, more than ever, he felt he had to find his mother. Not for one moment did he doubt that the words, "hers and …" would have been followed by the name Don Davenport. That his father could be in a triumvirate with the other two now made perfect sense; they fake his death, hold a virtual funeral and tell everyone only they will attend, because it's what Paul wanted. Then they buy a dodgy death certificate from a corrupt official. Then they get the loot. Maybe they didn't even bother with a death certificate; Danny was away at the time and Sharon was living with a weird boyfriend in a 'Goth' commune in Whitby. His father had to be party to defrauding the sisters and the rest of the family. Who blackmailed whom? Well, a lawyer and an accountant, working hand-in-glove, would know how to set things up, particularly if offered a slice of an inheritance estimated at one hundred million pounds. Danny felt sick. He rushed to the lavatory and only just made it. After four retches he began to recover and went back to his chair to mull over what had brought that on. Perhaps it was the trauma of seeing his father die in front of him compounded by the fact that he had obviously colluded in a massive and appalling fraud to the detriment of his own family. He was almost pleased that it appalled him. At least he still possessed a moral compass in spite of his dodgy genetic legacy.

★★★★★

Justyn tapped his forefinger on the steering wheel, waiting impatiently at the top of the road. Danny spotted him, swung open the passenger side door and slumped into the seat. He laid his hands on the dashboard, as if offering a prayer, sweating profusely.

Justyn turned to him.

"You alright, mate?"

"Yeah, well sort of. You wait twenty years to meet your dead father and just when you start to get over the shock he's still alive, he really does die!"

"Before anyone could say 'how's your father?' " Danny laughed at Justyn's joke, grateful for some light relief.

"I'm slowly piecing it together. Mum and Dad, with Davenport's help, blackmail Ken Stone, defraud the others and fake Dad's death so they all massively gain financially, but Dad has to *really* disappear. Mum distracts us with lies whilst disappearing herself, but not to the place she told us about in Mallorca. Then she tells us not to contact her, but she'll contact us. We see her from time to time in England, but are told not to look for her in Mallorca."

"Funny how your Mum and Davenport, then your Dad, all alight upon Mallorca."

"Why?"

"Well, wouldn't it have been easier to split up, geographically I mean? Would have been harder to track them down."

"Maybe, but let's face it, Dad and Davenport, being accountant and solicitor respectively, probably deemed it simpler to set up new identities and residencies in the same place. They could vouch for each other. It's also likely they didn't trust each other – keep your friends close, your enemies closer!"

"A very elaborate hoax for a mess of pottage?"

"What do you mean?"

Justyn bit his lip, hesitating before answering, wondering whether to share his thoughts with Danny at such a sensitive time. He decided against it. He kept thinking it didn't make sense, something darker must be going on. In his mind money alone would not be a sufficient reason to disappear or fake your own death.

"Hmmm – doesn't say much for those professions, does it? Probably why I decided to be a rock star." His words didn't reflect his thoughts.

"Tried to be a rock star!" Danny shot him a reproachful look.

"Yeah, well, tried, failed, whatever … at least I didn't shaft my own flesh and blood." Justyn glanced across and saw tears welling up in Danny's eyes. "Oh sorry, very tactless of me …"

Silence engulfed them until Danny recovered: "Drive on."

"It doesn't make sense though," Justyn wouldn't let go.

"What?"

"What's going on. All this subterfuge, faking death, changing identities." Hearing no response, Justyn decided to keep his thoughts to himself.

As they turned into the hotel car park, Justyn cursed. He could see Horace and Guy sitting by the pool: Horace, heavy and wheezing, Guy looking ill at ease. He didn't know which of them annoyed him more. Clare was nowhere to be seen.

"Back to the odd couple." Justyn said grumpily.

"We still don't know who attacked Davenport in the car park at Valldemossa."

"And we don't know where Davenport is now."

"Are you scared?"

"Yes, Justyn, I am scared. Very scared. I've wrecked their plans. Nobody wanted me to find Dad, least of all him. I can't find Mum,

Davenport could hire a hitman to get me for all I know – or the guy who put the frighteners on him may come after me." He paused. "I could be next! I probably am next!" He felt his skin go clammy. They exchanged glances but were distracted by a navy blue Golf revving past them out of the car park. The driver, eyes hidden behind large sunglasses, offered no acknowledgement. Danny shrugged dismissively. Justyn looked alarmed.

"Did you see who was driving?"

"No, who?"

"Clare!"

"So?"

"Why the hell's she blanking us? Why's she blanking *me*?"

★★★★★

The crumpled map laid out on the passenger seat was too big and unwieldy for Clare to read as she drove towards Palma so she stopped at a petrol station and parked out of the way. She was not at all sure she was doing the right thing.

A couple of days earlier she had got chatting to a man in the bar at the hotel. His name was Pablo and it turned out he was a retired Mallorcan *policía*. He had been recently widowed and Clare could tell that he was lonely and keen to talk. Just to make conversation she asked him whether there was much crime on the island and was astonished when he launched into lurid tales about drug cartels and money launderers. She had a feeling he might be exaggerating and decided to call his bluff by asking where these people could be found. Without missing a beat he reeled off the names of bars and night clubs where, for the right money you could get pretty much anything you wanted. As he was talking an idea began to grow in her mind. And now here she was on her way to explore a shady world that she knew nothing about.

Satisfied with the route, she folded up the map and decided to carry on to Playa de Palma; a scrunched scrap of paper on her dashboard bore the names of two nightclubs. It was early evening and as she drove through the tree lined streets of Playa de Palma she envied all the holiday-makers ambling along or sitting having a drink in the pavement cafés. She also caught sight of the beach with its pointy sun shades that look like trees and longed for the moment when she and Justyn could spend a day swimming and sunbathing, rather than locked in this horrible nightmare.

Two or three miles out of the resort she spotted a bright pink building with a flashing neon sign saying Mimi's Disco. This must be it. It looked like an old cinema that had been converted into a nightclub. She pulled onto the deserted forecourt. She was beginning to lose her nerve and half hoped it would be closed, but a large man in a crumpled uniform came over to her.

"Puedo estacionar tu auto?"

She felt perfectly able to park the car herself, but suspected it would be unwise to decline.

"Si. Gracias." She smiled politely and handed over the keys.

Nervously, Clare left the bright sunshine. She pulled open the heavy door to the building and was plunged into darkness. It took a while for her eyes to adjust. She was in what would have been the foyer of the cinema but now it was thickly carpeted and lit only by thin strips of neon around the edge of the floor and ceiling. There was a black shiny reception desk embellished with gold trim but no one was behind it. She was about to turn and flee when the door into the club opened and out came a tall man who she guessed might be Middle Eastern. His shirt was unbuttoned almost to his waist and there was a clutch of gold medallions hanging round his neck. She found herself lost for words. The man came over and stood just a bit too close to her:

"A beautiful lady on her own. Are you here for good time, beautiful lady?"

She could smell whisky on his breath.

"I'm on holiday, actually."

"Oh, nice, with husband or maybe away from husband?"

"I'm looking for someone who could, you know, do a sort of job for me."

"Wait there. You need the Argentinian."

He walked over to the entrance to the club and as he opened the door Clare caught a glimpse of the interior. It was huge and on different levels. On the highest she spotted a girl rehearsing her pole dance routine. The man returned a few minutes later with another man who he introduced as Osvaldo. He was small and thick set and when he smiled he flashed a gold front tooth.

"Osvaldo, this nice lady wants someone to do a 'fix'."

"I'm not sure I want a 'fix'. I certainly don't want drugs!"

"Well, lady …"

"I have a name …"

"And it is?"

"Brigit," she lied.

"I think we should sit down." Osvaldo motioned towards a table tucked in the corner.

"So, Lady Brigit, what can your new friend, Osvaldo, do for you?"

"I need to find someone. Well, two people actually." She thought she sounded ridiculous.

"Tell me about them. Where are they from? How old are they?"

Clare looked uncomfortably around her.

"They're English and quite old."

"Can you show me picture of old people?"

Clare pulled out a picture of Don Davenport and her Aunt Alison from her handbag, explaining it was twenty years old, but they wouldn't have changed much. They looked old even then.

Osvaldo shook his head, "No. I can't help you with this."

"Why not?"

"I just can't. You must find someone else."

"If it's a question of money, that needn't be a problem."

"No I'm sorry. It's out of the question. Is that not so, Mahmoud?"

Clare thought that perhaps this was all a bit too low level for the likes of them and dropped the photograph back into her handbag. She was almost relieved. It was a very silly idea after all. She thanked the two men for their time and hurried across the foyer to the exit.

It was a shock to be back in the blinding sunshine after the gloom of the club and Clare reached into her bag for her sunglasses. The concierge was waiting and sidled up to her.

"Tu coche?"

"Si, por favor."

While she waited for the car she realised how stupid she'd been. What on earth did she think she was playing at trying to hire local gangsters? What was happening to her? She was just wondering what she would say to Justyn, when her car pulled up. The concierge made no move to get out. He stared at her and Clare suddenly felt alone and very vulnerable. This was not a world of please and thank you but a place where only money talked. She reached for her wallet and pulled out a twenty euro note. It was a lot of money for parking a car, but she felt scared and just wanted to get away. The concierge laughed and got out of the car. She had never felt so humiliated.

Once back behind the wheel, she put up the sun visor as the sun was now dipping behind the buildings. Turning on the lights she set off on the return journey to Deià. Before long, the black silhouettes of the Tramuntana Mountains calmed her and she began to think again about what she was going to tell Justyn; she knew he'd seen her leave. When she eventually pulled into the hotel car park, he was there, waiting for her. She tried desperately to appear normal and smiled, but Justyn was having none of it.

"So what's going on Clare?" She felt the chill, having irrationally hoped for 'Clarezy'. He stared at her as if she had just burgled his house. She tried but failed to speak and brushed past him, still too confused and ashamed to know what to say.

"Look, I don't want to fall out. We've only just got back together."

"I know, JS," she paused, "but I just can't tell you much at the moment. I need to see Mum. Just cut me a bit of slack, please?"

A peal of goat bells on the hillside accompanied her to the hotel entrance. Justyn paused knowing it heralded a storm brewing, but he went back to the pool anyway. Later, from his sun lounger, he saw Clare return to her car, having showered and changed. Shaking his head, he decided against challenging her again. She suspected he was watching her. She spread the map out across the steering wheel. Frowning, she weighed up her options. She could either head back via Valldemossa towards Palma then north near Santa Maria, but decided instead to cross the entire loop of the Tramuntana, to Pollença. She had travelled this route before and had found it calming. Earlier in the day her mother had phoned and suggested they meet for a drink at sundown in the market square under some ancient orange trees, making it clear she wouldn't be inviting her sister, Diana. On the route through Sóller, up the steep winding roads past the hippy markets of Estellenes and Fornalutz, she began to tremble; roller skaters with night lamps attached to their helmets flanked each side of her and she could see exactly how Grant Morrison could have crashed off the road. Slowing down, exhausted, she pulled into a car park near the market square and checked her watch; it had taken thirty minutes longer than she thought. She was feeling calmer but couldn't see any sign of her mother in the bar. She ordered a Diet

Coke and asked the waiter if an elderly lady had been in by herself?

"No, sorry." came the curt reply.

Clare, shielded her eyes, scanning the other bars and restaurants lining the market square, all with candles flickering on the tables. It was all so congenial and pretty and she felt cross that yet again she wasn't able to have a good time here. There was no one resembling her mother but she did notice an elderly couple chatting in a far corner. They were over twenty yards away but she had a spooky feeling that she was looking at Alison Galvin and Don Davenport. As she got to her feet to rush across to them she heard a clipped English voice.

"Ah, there you are Clare, and about time too!" Her mother embraced her, sighing affectionately.

"So great to see you Mum," her words raced out.

"Clare, what's up? You seem so stressed. Calm down."

"They're over there," Clare blurted, "Aunt Alison and Davenport. Over there."

"I don't see anyone darling."

Neither could Clare. They had gone.

★★★★★

"The female of the species is far deadlier than the male." Kipling's words played in Justyn's head as he tried to fathom what Clare had been up to and why she wasn't being honest with him. He really thought they would make it this time, that she was The One for the rest of his life. But she was being elusive again. Where was she now? It was getting late but he was still sitting by the pool watching cars coming and going in the car park. He looked hopefully over the hedge as another vehicle entered the car park, but it wasn't Clare's blue Golf. He was just about to turn round and go back to the hotel when he caught sight of a grey Citröen he had noticed earlier, parked under a gnarled old olive tree, as if trying to hide. He thought he could see a figure sitting in the driving seat. Danny had fallen asleep on his sun lounger but Justyn couldn't resist waking him.

"Danny. Danny. There's a guy in a grey Citröen parked over there. I think he's keeping some sort of watch." Danny, half-asleep, grunted and dragged himself up to follow Justyn's gaze.

"Valldemossa man?"

"Could be, but where the hell's Clare?" The question was more directed at her brother but he was also asleep, snoring gently. Horace *really* got on his nerves.

"Horace. Where's Clare?" Horace jolted awake. "What did you say?"

"Where's Clare?"

"She's gone to see Mum somewhere in Pollença; Guy's gone to see his mother, Diana. Could've gone together." Justyn nodded, still watching the stranger in the car park.

"I'll go and have a chat with him." Before he could put his sandals on, they heard the engine start up and the Citröen quickly drove off. The driver swerved right onto the main road, twisting his head back round to look at them.

"Probably a drug dealer, waiting for someone," Horace suggested. "In fact I think I may have seen him before."

"How come, Horace?"

"Shortly after I flew in, there was someone behind me in the car hire queue who seemed a bit too interested in where I was going."

"Did he follow you from the airport?" Justyn asked anxiously.

"I'm not sure." Horace replied nonchalantly. "But I do remember seeing him get into a grey Citröen."

"Well, it wasn't Valldemossa man, unless he'd changed cars," Danny interrupted, "he wouldn't have got there in time anyway, if he was trailing Horace to Palma. Unless he left when I did. I suppose he could have been tracking me to get to Don Davenport."

Justyn's phone rang. It was Clare.

"Hi, it's me." She sounded coquettish.

"Yes?" No sound came back. "Yes, what is it, Clarezy?"

There was a scream and the line went dead.

★★★★★

Clare had kissed her mother goodbye and returned to her seat. As she ambled away Clare was struck by how old and frail she looked. She had never, until now, thought of her mother as old, but it suddenly struck her that before long she would need to be cared for and their relationship would change. After all, she herself was now approaching middle age. Her long and unstable relationship with Justyn had meant she had never had children and she began to wonder who would care for *her* when the time came. But this wasn't the time or place to be worrying about all that; right now she just wanted all this family trauma to end so that at least her mother could find some peace and contentment and they could all go back to their normal lives.

She was jolted out of all these thoughts by a figure standing by her table. Her heart skipped a beat when she realised it was Osvaldo the Argentinian she'd met at Playa de Palma. A small, squat fellow with a large scar running from his left eye to the corner of his mouth stood next to him. She grabbed her phone and called Justyn. Just as he answered, Osvaldo lunged towards her and she screamed.

"Miss Brigit." Osvaldo clasped his hand over Clare's mouth. Her face reddened, but she decided to trust her instinct and stay put rather than fight back.

"Be quiet. We won't hurt you. Now pretend we friends." She

nodded as they took seats on either side of her. Osvaldo calmly ordered two coffees from the concerned-looking waiter. A couple, dressed in hiking gear, approached their table.

"Sorry to interfere," the man said in the clear, confident tones of the Englishman abroad, "but are you alright? We heard a fearful scream." For a moment Clare hesitated but she mumbled, "Yes, old friends. I was surprised to see them here, such a joy, this is Osvaldo and this is … " They didn't wait to hear the second name. They nodded their approval and moved away.

"You see Miss Brigit," Osvaldo looked intently at her, "you mess with things that much better you don't mess with, don't you agree, Diego?"

Diego nodded. "No mess with things, Miss."

Clare turned, studying the short, squat man again, wondering how and when he had been scarred.

"Not good for Miss to mess!" Osvaldo shot a look of disapproval at his accomplice. He was going beyond his remit, which was merely to agree with his boss.

"Who are you?" Clare demanded.

"You know who we are, you find us yourself."

"Yes, but who are you working for? Why wouldn't you help me? What's going on?"

"We don't want trouble from you. We can't tell you what we do and who we do it for."

"I'd rather assumed that." Clare relaxed a little, anxious to keep her new South American friends talking.

"No, I understand, I won't make trouble, I won't mess." Osvaldo smirked, feeling pleased with himself. He pushed his chair back from the table and sprang to his feet.

"We go, we hope we don't see you again!" Diego swiftly followed suit.

It began to dawn on Clare that they may already be looking for Don and Alison. That would explain their blank refusal to help her and the fact that they were trying to frighten her off. On second thoughts she decided that it was all too far fetched and she was letting her imagination get the better of her. Her phone pinged. It was a text from Justyn: *Are you in Pollença? Am on my way. Text me back if not in the market square."* Clare waited, fidgeting in her seat. As darkness fell the bars and restaurants started to fill up. Chairs screeched on hard floors, friends greeted each other, laughter soon filled the market square. Justyn's rolling gait came into view. He was carrying his helmet under his arm. Spotting her, he hurried, trying to run, nervous about the response he would receive. Clare stood up as he raised his arms in greeting. She buried her face in his chest.

"I'm so pleased to see you." She began to cry.

"It's Okay, it's Okay. Whatever it is, it's Okay. I'm here. We're together."

"They're watching us, let's go."

"What on earth's going on?" Justyn turned to her, his face pinched with anxiety.

"We can't talk here JS. Two guys who've just put the frighteners on me are still lurking around."

"What? Why on earth … ? D'you want to head back to Deià or go somewhere else?" He took her hand.

"Deià. I need the calm of the Tramuntana."

"Let's not lose each other again!" He ran his hand tenderly over her shoulder and pulled her to him, hugging her tight. "Whatever's been going on, we stick together now."

Clare's large brown eyes rendered him helpless. He wondered if he would ever truly understand this complicated woman. She'd obsessed him for over twenty years but now at fifty-eight he was desperate to settle down and spend the rest of his life with her. These were his thoughts as he drove his motorbike behind her Golf along the fast road back to Santa Maria.

He was startled by a huge swish of air and a loud noise. A Mercedes Sports car travelling at about twice the speed he was, overtook, going as near to him as it possibly could, without knocking him off the bike. He felt slammed by a wall of displaced air. Then he watched in horror as it almost scraped the side of Clare's car, before racing away. Justyn held back, controlling his natural instinct to chase after it, knowing he had the power to, but fearing a trap. Clare indicated right, and slowed to pull over into a layby. Dutifully he braked and followed her.

"Jesus! That was close! Who the hell d'you think they were?" He removed his helmet, but before he could say any more, Clare wrapped her arms around his waist, breaking down again, tears rolling down her cheeks. He stood holding her, soothing her, giving her time to regain control.

"I will … tell you all … I really don't want to have secrets from you, JS, to hide things from you … but not today. I can't today." He shook his head, exasperated.

"Why not?"

"I'm on someone's radar and if we, or more likely you, do anything now, it would only make matters worse." She stopped sobbing but was still shaking. Tenderly, Justyn hugged her closer.

"Look, Clarezy, people can't go putting the frighteners on you and get away with it. I'll …"

"That's the point, JS, you'll do something, I know you too well. You'll do something rash, something brave but probably …" hesitating, looking away from him, "not helpful." Pulling back from his embrace, she gave him a tender look, almost smiling through her tears at Justyn's confused expression.

"So, when will you tell me?"

"Maybe later, if you're a good boy and …" he was relieved to see the seductive look he knew so well, he was even more certain: 'The female of the species is far deadlier than the male.' Justyn heard his phone ping. Seeing a missed call from Danny, he hurriedly pressed redial.

"Hi, where are you guys?" Danny sounded anxious.

"Double parked on the edge of life!" Justyn joked, "me and my main bitch, Clare Loosemore!" Danny didn't laugh.

Justyn straightened his back, asking "Okay, what's going on?"

"I now know more about what's going on. A lot more. Let's meet for supper. The upstairs tapas restaurant in the town? I'll book – 8 p.m." Danny hung up. Justyn gripped Clare's hand and suggested they got on with the journey to Deià. Clare smiled, nodding in agreement.

★★★★★

Danny sat forward waiting impatiently for Justyn and Clare to join him at the restaurant. He had spent nearly all day dealing with a lot of red tape concerning his father's death. So many agencies were involved: doctors, civil servants and, of course, the *policía*. It was going to take months to sort out and he was going to have to find his father's passport and documents before the body could be released. There was so much he didn't know. Was there a fake death certificate for his previous disappearance or had he just assumed an alias? Danny decided he would need Sharon to help him, but he hadn't even had the courage to tell her yet that not only had her father been alive, but was now dead again. It would be funny if it wasn't so appalling. Before long he saw Clare and Justyn heading towards his table on the balcony overlooking the square.

"Where are the odd couple?" Justyn tried to lighten the atmosphere.

"Dunno, haven't seen them since early afternoon, don't think it's a big problem! So, where have Bonnie and Clyde been today?" Clare sighed, hoping Justyn didn't immediately reply. He raised his arm in the air, as if hailing a taxi, and ordered a beer.

"Well, it's been one hell of a day." Unsure where to start, Justyn chose a distraction: "You know your grandfather, Ken Stone?"

"Yes, but it's a bit random to suddenly bring him up isn't it?" Clare shot Justyn a concerned glance.

"Well, I've been thinking about him quite a lot lately. It was something dear old Hector said, a couple of days before he drowned. It keeps playing on my mind." Clare ran her fingers down the menu, wondering where he was going with this. "You know Hector was terrified of him, of your grandfather."

"Why?" Danny sounded matter-of-fact, almost indifferent.

"He'd worked for him, apparently from the age of about thirteen, as an apprentice of some sort, on the landscape gardening side of things." Danny nodded in agreement. Clare swallowed hard.

"I remember Mum telling us that once when we were in Cornwall back in the '70s that she thought Hector was a bit weird."

Irritated, Justyn replied, "I'd say he was and with good reason. Did you know that your Grandfather sexually abused him over quite a long time?" Danny didn't respond. He was looking absently over the balcony at a group of loud British tourists discussing where they were going for dinner.

"He was a control freak." Clare, her face pale and serious, slowly looked up from her menu, deciding it was time to share information about this skeleton from her family's cupboard. Now she was ready to join in. "He had what's called a narcissistic personality. It's a disorder caused by an inflated sense of self-worth."

"I can think of a few people with that!" Danny smiled.

"Not to that degree. You see he didn't have any sort of empathy for others. He was incredibly vain and dominated everyone around him. It's a personality type. I've studied it."

"I forgot you did that psychology degree." Clare never ceased to surprise Justyn and some of the emotional ambivalence he had felt about her that day began to fall away.

"Yes, and I used my grandfather for my thesis, as a case study. I'd seen the emotional damage he'd wreaked on his family. His need for control was total. He had a superiority complex and that type don't care who they trample to get what they feel they deserve."

Danny looked shocked: "So you think he damaged the whole family?"

"Oh yes." Clare held his gaze.

"Without wishing to upset you Danny, how come your mum and Davenport managed to manipulate him? I mean how would he have allowed that?" Justyn waved away the waiter who had come to take their order.

"They blackmailed him!" Clare and Danny replied in unison.

Justyn was taken aback.

"They blackmailed him." Danny repeated, lowering his voice, dropping his head, looking down at the table, as if it could provide him with some comfort or inspiration. "Some time before his terminal illness set in they made their move, blackmailing him about going public with his abuse of Hector Wallace and others. I've worked out what happened. Had my father returned to my life for more than a brief cameo role, I'm sure he would have told me a lot more about it. I know he was ready to. You see, Mum and Dad knew about his abuse of Hector, and remember, Davenport had been on the scene for decades, he knew all about it too."

"I see." Justyn shook his head, took a swig of his beer and wiped his mouth with the back of his hand.

"Do you?" Danny challenged Justyn, as he shot a glance at Clare, wondering whether to change the subject. What did she think? He needed her help.

"I caught them together one August afternoon in 1972." Justyn paused, "I was looking for Dad's art gallery in St Ives. They didn't see me. Davenport had got off the bus and your mum, Danny, was waiting in a café by that triangular bus stop in the town."

"I never knew that."

"I guess he took the bus so his wife could have the car for the afternoon." Danny, nodded meekly in agreement.

"You see, the character type Stone was ..." Clare interrupted. Justyn stared at her. This was the first time he'd ever heard her refer to her grandfather by his surname. Then it dawned on him, he had never actually heard her talk about him at all. He went back to listening to what she had to say.

"He not only craved subordination from others, but had to receive it. His type can't cope with being reviled or rejected in any way. They have to be 'top dog' at all times."

"So it's not hard to guess how the three of them played out the blackmail," Justyn concluded.

"Yeah, well, Dad always chased money, particularly thinking his father-in-law regarded him as a disappointment – and mum, now it would seem, just wanted a new life with Davenport," Danny struggled, his voice trailing off.

"They all wanted a new life, and they worked out how to finance it. Still, it doesn't really make sense to throw out your old life, move abroad and in your dad's case, Danny, fake his own death, change identity, bury the past – all just for money. Sorry, there's got to be more to it. I'm sure of it." Justyn's voice was getting louder and he was almost shouting as he began to grapple with all the pieces in the jigsaw.

It was becoming cooler and as Clare turned to get her cardigan from the back of her chair she was distracted by something beneath the balcony.

CHAPTER SIX

Guy had first noticed her earlier in the year when he travelled to Mallorca to check out the route his cycling team would take on their fund-raising event in September. She seemed to pop up everywhere in Deià: waitressing in the beachside restaurant, stacking shelves in the very narrow aisles of the supermarket, even helping out with housekeeping at the hotel where he was staying. Everyone seemed to know her. He thought he heard her name was pronounced as 'Laya'. And now he saw her walking ahead of him on the twisting road leading down to the rocky beach, he was sure she had turned round more than once to check he was still following.

The weather that day was unsure of itself. The wind was warm but a storm seemed a strong possibility with dark clouds sweeping across the sky. Guy took a seat in the beachside café, enjoying watching the crash of the waves. Suddenly she was there in front of him. Her dark hair was cut into a short bob that framed an almost perfect oval face. Her eyes were green with a hint of sadness. He ordered a café solo and tried to imagine her life. He watched her slalom between tables filling with mid-morning coffee drinkers, admiring her long-limbed, softly curved figure. Listening carefully, he tried to trace her accent. It sounded hybrid Anglo-Spanish.

Guy began to reflect on his own life and decided it was all his father's fault that things hadn't worked out for him. He had never shown him any affection and, as he was an only child, it was a source of bitterness to Guy and bewilderment to all those who witnessed it. He was prone to temper tantrums and his mother, on more than one occasion, had rushed to his school after a summons from the headmaster. She knew he wasn't a happy child. He had grown too fast and his wide sticking out ears, had earned him the unfortunate nickname 'Elephant Boy.'

Unbeknown to him, the lack of affection extended to his mother's life too. By the time he was in his teens he was all too aware of Diana's unhappiness. Restless and uncomfortable at their suburban home, she looked for any excuse to be out in the evenings, forever joining new clubs, societies, committees. Guy would keep to his room after school, while his father, Donald, would arrive home, pleading exhaustion from running his one man insurance business, and slump down in his designated chair in the sitting room to watch endless detective series on TV.

Guy rebelled by sculpting his hair with gel into a spike and by playing punk rock, thumping on the floor in his Doc Martens, as The Jam roared 'We come from places you don't want to go'. Many times he thought of running away and half-suspected his father wanted him to.

After messing up his 'A' Levels, his father's only comment was, "Don't know why you bothered taking them." At nineteen Guy had a Damascene moment and applied to join the SAS. To everyone's surprise, he got in. Diana was startled at the way it transformed him almost overnight. His father didn't even notice as, a few years before Guy was commissioned, he'd left the family home. He moved in with a mousy librarian with Nana Mouskouri spectacles, who had a one bedroom flat above the library. It was the most radical thing he ever did. Without his father, Guy had less to be angry about and his mother was now free of the monosyllabic tyrant who had dominated her life for so many years. Guy suspected for a while that she had a lover. He couldn't blame her, but was shocked when he later discovered the extent of her extra-marital affairs. In the meantime he channelled his anger into his new military career, becoming obsessed with passing out as the best in class.

Nine years later, when he left the SAS, he struggled to settle down, both personally and professionally. His one serious relationship with Marian ended painfully when she wrote to him while he was in Afghanistan to inform him she was now engaged to someone else. He would never forget that day. He felt bitter and let down and his attitude towards women changed. They were duplicitous and untrustworthy and he moved from one casual encounter to another, referring to them as 'conquests,' in boastful texts to his friends.

He eventually settled in Bedford, where he didn't know anyone but could play up his SAS background. In the end he found a job selling financial services. He recoiled at the thought of being a 'chip off the old block,' but knew he was following a bit of a genetic line. He joined UKIP and immersed himself in local politics and tried but failed to become a town councillor. Only when he took up cycling did he find an appropriate release for his unspent energy. As he reflected on his past life, he felt a terrible sense of failure.

He was awoken from his reverie by Leia as she placed his café solo on the table in front of him. When she smiled a gap between her two front teeth did nothing to diminish her charm.

"Thanks."

"Thank you."

"Um, just a moment, can I ask you, is it safe to swim here?"

"Of course, but not in this weather." Both laughed hearing the wind rise, looking out to see the fury of the tide crashing on the rocks. For a brief moment he held her gaze, certain her eyes were now smiling too.

"Thanks." she turned, moving to the next table. Before she spoke to the customers there, she coyly glanced back. Briefly their eyes met again.

★★★★★

Danny was surprised when he spotted Guy with a rather beautiful woman on an oppressively hot afternoon in Valldemossa. He had parked his car and was heading to the office of Martin Whitlock, just off the high street. He was eager to meet the solicitor acting for the estate of his father but was stopped in his tracks when he saw Guy walking out of a gift shop hand in hand with this female. He looked away and pretended he hadn't seen them. He decided he would ask the others if they knew he was seeing someone.

Monika had given Danny Whitlock's details with what he felt was a rather disconcerting enthusiasm for them to meet as soon as possible.

Monika had said, "He's nice man, fiftyish."

Whitlock opened the door seeing Danny approach. He had obviously been waiting for him. He stuck out a hand. He was a short stocky man with a thick head of honey-coloured hair and pale blue eyes and appeared rather younger than his years.

"Do take your jacket off, it's a scorcher today and the aircon's playing up!"

As they went into a small conference room, Danny felt a line of sweat building on his forehead. Whitlock appeared nervous and wasted no time on preliminaries.

"I'll be candid, your father made two wills, one was a trust, the other one was personal. Sorry, I should have said how sorry I am for your loss." The solicitor sounded too matter of fact and insincere for

Danny's liking. He was immediately on his guard.

"Thank you. Before you start, I discovered my father had changed his identity." Martin looked down, offering no response. Danny continued:

"Are the wills in the name of Galvin or Beal?"

"They are in his original name."

"Are you aware of the name change?"

"Yes, he did tell me."

"Didn't you think it odd?" Danny challenged Whitlock, watching him stiffen a little. A silence fell, Whitlock looked down at his hands.

"Alright, let's leave that subject for the moment," Whitlock sighed, relieved.

"How did the trust one work?"

"He did this will with an associate, the two of them were trustees." Danny shifted in his seat. He could now guess the rest.

"Who was that associate?"

"Donald Davenport." They both said the name together, after the solicitor started the first syllable of the first name. Danny helped answer his own question.

"Who are the beneficiaries?"

"Your mother and her partner, Don Davenport."

"And the second one?"

"There are only two beneficiaries."

Danny waited.

"Mr Daniel Galvin and Ms Sharon Galvin."

Whitlock drew himself up to his full height, sticking out his hand to shake Danny's who rebuffed him with a wave of the arm.

"Which will do you think will prevail?"

"I'm sure the new one will prevail, as is customary, the only reason I haven't thrown out the first one is that I've been trying to get hold of Mr Davenport to explain. In my opinion the first one, the trust, could be challenged anyway. It's irregular, quite unusual for a solicitor to be a beneficiary, particularly if he's instrumental in setting up the trust and is also a trustee. I've never come across it before; it could be argued that the will is unfairly detrimental to the deceased's family. But, in any event, I'm bound by precedent to ensure a new will revokes all previous wills. We can get Counsel's advice, but I was never happy with the trust one anyway, merely taking delivery of it, some twenty years ago. You see Mr Davenport dealt with it and as the solicitor responsible he merely handed it to me as a *fait accompli* to register it. Do you understand?"

"Yes, I do, I understand very well, Mr Whitlock. Don Davenport is a very nasty piece of work. He manipulated my grandfather's will, benefiting my mother, defrauding her sisters, and so it would appear, all his other relations." Danny paused, unsure how much more to say. Should he admit Pat and Diana were here on the island now, together with their children, hunting down Davenport and Danny's mother?

"I rather suspected as much, even though I never actually met Davenport." Danny stared at him.

"What?"

"Well, Davenport contacted me from time to time, checking things were in order as originally instructed. Your father was very wary of Mr Davenport. He told me to always do what he said and not to cross him. To tell you the truth, Danny, I think he was afraid of him."

"How much contact did you have with my father? Did you meet him often?"

"Oh yes, many times. Quite a lot recently. He seemed very vexed about how things had turned out."

"So, when did Dad make this personal will?" Danny half-smiled, feeling able to refer to his father as such again.

"Very recently."

"How recently?"

"Last week. The day before he died." Whitlock's piercing blue eyes caused Danny to shift in his seat.

"Could that be a problem? I mean could Davenport challenge its validity as it was made literally the day before he died?"

"Possibly, Davenport might well try to do so."

"It could flush him out. "

"I'm sorry?"

"He's gone to ground you see, Martin – may I call you Martin? Davenport and my mother are in hiding."

"How do you know? Who's searching for them?"

Danny didn't answer, taking stock of the man whose help he now very much needed. He knew Whitlock would revoke the first will, he was only surprised he hadn't done so already, but he also felt that at last he had found someone he could trust.

"I am and so are my cousins and their mothers, we're all searching for them. We're all here on the island. Have been for over a week. Davenport stitched us all up, by manipulating Mum, his partner, even Dad. He duped them all into blackmailing my grandfather, Ken Stone."

Whitlock didn't react but concentrated on scribbling some notes.

"Go on …" Danny couldn't. His mouth had dried up. But he managed to ask "How much are we talking about?"

Surprised at the sudden directness of Danny's question, Whitlock hesitated, cleared his throat. "Um, about thirty …"

"Thirty thousand pounds?"

"No, thirty million, thirty million pounds."

CHAPTER SEVEN

Guy Roope had a problem. He drank too much. He needed to drink, particularly in the evenings. After he left the army a counsellor had tried to help him.

"You know you have a problem Guy. You need to confront it." Guy's inner voice yelled 'get stuffed', but his actual reply was:

"And that is?"

"You have a problem with commitment, in part due to your parents' behaviour, and your unhappy childhood. You run away from things, and then you drink."

'Well, waddayouknow?' he thought. *You give consultants your watch, they tell you the time, then they give it back, charging you for the privilege.* It was how he felt about the shrink who was trying to help him now. He also knew he couldn't delude himself anymore. His drinking was getting worse. He was sure his first pouring of Johnnie Walker Double Black continued a little longer into the tumbler each time he poured. It soothed him and he knew it was probably Okay if he left it at that. But he never did. Far too soon his hand would once again reach for the neck of the bottle. He was more controlled in company, careful to ensure no one would know he had a drink problem. But he knew it. He also knew, in all aspects of his life, he had learnt to act out different roles. He was very accomplished at fooling people, but he couldn't fool himself.

Soon after he had chatted to Leia in the beach café, he dreamt of her. He was travelling towards Sóller across rutted and hazardous terrain. As he descended towards an isolated cove he saw a figure stripping off near the rocks. To his delight he recognised Leia. When he slipped slightly on broken ground, disturbing stones, she turned and saw him. He was sure he saw her smile.

"Why don't you join me?" The gap tooth was further proof that it was her. He bounded forward, feasting his eyes on the beauty of her naked body. Then he woke up. His dream told him his mission. He got up, skipped his usual morning routine of forty press-ups and headed straight to the shower. Invigorated by the hot water powering down, and recalling his dream, he scrubbed with an even greater zeal than usual. He had to have Leia, but this time, he told himself, he would have to behave properly, treat her respectfully, not abandon her as just another conquest. He even surprised himself by hoping that Leia could make him a better person.

Leia, for her part, had begun to think more about the charismatic Englishman who on several recent occasions had crossed her path. She was sure he wasn't a tourist, or even a conventional sort of person. Was he twice her age? Instinctively she thought the man was a risk, possibly high risk. But he was energizing, intoxicating. Her hippy Australian mother would have admired her free spirit. She wondered what her father would have said, but she'd never known him. She didn't even know who he was.

It wasn't long before Roope made his move and took Leia on a walk down to the beach where he had dreamed of finding her naked. Accompanied by the gentle drone of cicadas and the faint chirping of birds, they meandered through cypress trees towards the rocks below. As the crystal clear ocean came into view, he led her to the secluded location he had chosen earlier that day. Leia recognised the scenario, smiling a little uncertainly. She had been here before, but still shivered as a frisson of anticipation gripped her. Soon she yielded to Guy's urgent embraces, and it wasn't long before she was lying beneath him, listening to whispered messages of undying love, staring beyond him at tall Mediterranean pines, replete with needle-laden branches.

★★★★★

The next day Leia suggested that they take a trip to Ibiza just for twenty-four hours. Her friend Carlos had a boat and he took tourists across from Puerto Portals. She wanted to take Guy to a club where they could stay up and dance all night. Digging him in the ribs, she had goaded him, "show me your stamina, old soldier man." Guy wasn't sure he liked the sound of all this, but Leia was full of life and he loved being with her. She relaxed him and at that moment he would have done anything to please her. He agreed that they would go to Puerto Portals to check out the boat although he knew he had to be back the following day for the big family reunion.

Nothing could have prepared Guy for the glamour of Puerto Portals. On the way to the marina they walked past expensive designer shops and glitzy restaurants and here he was with a pretty girl on his arm feeling for the first time in his life that things could work out. He had never been happier although he had a nagging feeling that it probably wouldn't last. They walked hand in hand past rows of huge super-yachts with liveried staff mopping the decks and they fantasised about where they would go if they could just climb aboard and cast off. Eventually the yachts gave way to more modest boats and wooden jetties.

"Oh. There's Carlos." Leia had spotted her friend standing by his boat at the end of the jetty. He was talking to an elderly couple. She started to walk down the jetty when Guy pulled her back.

"What's the matter?"

"I think I know those people talking to your friend."

"Well let's go and see them. What a coincidence!"

"No! You stay here." Leia felt alarmed by Guy's sudden change of mood and decided not to argue with him.

He walked down the jetty but stopped before he reached the boat and pretended to admire the view. He then paused and pulled out his phone. Guy thought the elderly woman looked rather like his Aunt Alison. It was extremely unlikely, but the closer he got the more sure he became that it was actually her. He presumed her companion must be Don Davenport. He could hardly believe his eyes and he was suddenly overwhelmed by an uncontrollable rage that drove everything else out of his head. He could just about make out enough of their conversation to learn that they were planning to take the boat at 11 a.m. the following day.

He walked slowly back to join Leia knowing that he couldn't now go on the trip to Ibiza with her, but unsure of precisely what to do next. He kissed her as tenderly as he could given the turmoil he was feeling, and then broke the news.

"Darling, I think it's best after all if you head back to Deià. I need to see my mother tonight in Pollença. I've just had a text from her. She seems upset. Let's go to Ibiza another time. You take the car back. I'll hire one here."

Leia was puzzled and searched his eyes for clues. Could she trust him or might he just get on the boat and abandon her?

"This isn't the end already, is it?" She started to break down, pummeling her fists on his tight chest. "Is it something to do with those people?"

"No. No, I promise. They're not who I thought they were. It's just my mum's only here for a short while. I've scarcely seen her." He surprised himself when he realised that this part, at least, was actually true. He took her hand in his, kissed it gently and smiled, trying to reassure her. Right now he needed to get this beautiful, trusting creature out of his life, at least for the next twenty four hours.

Dejected, Leia left, casting a glance through smudged mascara back over her shoulder at Guy. She fought back the tears. This wasn't the usual dumping – she'd had a few of those – this was a humiliation. She decided against returning to Deià. After all, the Melias had given her the day off. She decided to visit a girl friend who lived in Puerto Portals, just up from the marina. She would stay the night and fully expected that Guy would leave the next day for Ibiza without her. The thought of him getting on that boat with Carlos rocked her to the core. She'd seen the look in Guy's eyes, a look that said 'I'll call' but it somehow lacked conviction.

Guy meanwhile, had been keeping an eye on Alison and Don Davenport as they slowly left the jetty. He was able to catch up with them as they made their painstakingly slow way back to their apartment above the marina. He realised he couldn't just hang around outside, so decided to hire a car. There were plenty of hire firms to choose from. He found one next to a supermercado and having hired the car, he popped into the store and bought a large bottle of whisky. He was soon back outside the apartment but this time under the cover of a Fiat 500. There were no parking restrictions so he could park close by and keep watch as long he needed to. He felt bad about Leia but hoped that as soon as all this was over he would be able to make it up to her. There was no way he could have told her what was going on – it was just too complicated and she probably wouldn't have believed him anyway. He also didn't want to put her in any danger.

Night was drawing in and the buildings around the marina began to fill with shadows. Guy had a long wait. It wasn't until shortly after 10 a.m. the following day that he got the break he was hoping for. There, in front of him was the decrepit figure of Alison Galvin emerging from the block. Dressed in a white raincoat buttoned up to the neck, she looked anxiously around her before turning left towards the shopping mall. As soon as Guy saw her leave, he took a large gulp of whisky, before placing the bottle carefully under his seat. He got out of the car and waited until she had turned the corner and was out of sight.

His first problem was how to gain access to the apartment. During the time he had been watching the block very few people had come and gone, so he assumed they were mostly holiday flats not currently let. He was preparing for another long wait when he spotted an elderly British ex pat coming down the stairs. He had to be British as he was wearing a blue blazer and pale slacks. Guy approached the front door and took his keys from his pocket and started sorting through them as if looking for the right one. He then fumbled and dropped the whole bunch on the floor. The ruse worked. The man obligingly held the door open for him. Guy nodded, pushing in quickly, avoiding eye contact.

"Many thanks. Another fine day."

Once inside, Guy scanned the letter boxes. From his earlier surveillance he knew his targets lived on the sixth floor. He'd seen Davenport leaning on the railings of the balcony, with what looked like a morning coffee. Guy took the lift to the sixth floor. With the benefit of his training and years of experience, he quickly located the most likely door, based on his view from the street. He knocked gently on the door.

"Back already, love?"

The voice was gravelly. Old. Guy was in luck. As soon as Davenport opened the door, he pushed him back and slammed the door shut with a backward kick. Davenport was slumped against the wall, in shock and struggling to place who on earth this man could be. There was something familiar about his huge frame and large ears. Then it came to him. It was Diana's brutish son. He knew he had trained with the SAS. He had seen photographs of him taken when he was younger but even after twenty years it was so obviously him. He tried to rally:

"Now look, soldier boy, I don't know what your problem is, but you should get out now, while you can. You don't want to mess with me, soldier boy." He tried to sound authoritative and for a moment Guy hesitated. This man looked younger than he had expected, probably in his mid-seventies and was powerfully built with broad shoulders. Davenport straightened himself for a fight. Guy, the taller by a few inches, grabbed him by the shoulders and forced him back across a narrow corridor into the kitchen.

"You're not playing with amateurs now," Davenport bluffed, breathing quickly. He began to sweat. This man could do him serious harm; an overpowering stench of alcohol swept over him as he was pushed against a kitchen cupboard.

"Look, you're upset. I can see you right. We can sort things out."

"Oh we can, can we?"

Roope slammed Davenport's hand in the kitchen drawer, and then watched him try to prise it open, in an attempt to get hold of a knife. He stepped back and kick-boxed Davenport, who doubled over, falling to the floor. He howled in agony, his head thumping onto the floor tiles. Roope, squatted down and thrust his face up against Davenport's.

"Who are you? Why did you cheat us?"

"Get out of my face and I'll tell you."

Guy relented and allowed Davenport to struggle to a sitting position. Guy slumped back and the two men sat on the floor with their backs against the kitchen cupboards. They were both breathing heavily, their shoulders slumped and legs sticking out in front of them like two discarded puppets.

"You'd better tell the whole story." Guy was trying to control his anger at this man who had caused so much trouble.

"You're Guy aren't you? Diana's son."

"That's right and you know why I'm here."

"Look Guy, things are so much more complicated than they seem and if you'll give me time I *will* be able to share it all, but, there's something else …"

"What?"

"Well, you know you asked who I am. Well this may come as a shock to you and you may not believe me, but there's no other way to say it. I am your biological father."

It was as if a switch was flicked in Guy's brain. The fact that this loathsome man could presume to be his father was the last straw. He lost control. A red mist engulfed him.

He grabbed Davenport by the neck and with the skill of a trained assassin throttled him quickly and efficiently. Davenport gurgled, desperately thumping his hands on the cold kitchen floor until all his strength was gone.

Everything went quiet as Guy contemplated what he had done. The silence was broken by a knock on the door.

"Is that you dear?" He tried to imitate Davenport's voice.

"You Okay in there old chap?" Guy released a slow breath, relieved it was not Alison. He presumed it was a nosey neighbour and groaned, as he moved the washing machine.

"Problems with the bloody washing machine. All sorted," he grunted. The machine squeaked loudly on the floor as he pushed it back. "Thanks for your concern."

"Okay. Glad you're alright. I'll be on my way."

Guy listened to his footsteps receding down the corridor and heard a door click shut. He checked Davenport had no pulse and pulled him along the corridor to the bedroom. Davenport was a big man and it took all of Guy's strength to heave the body onto the bed. He covered it with the pink floral duvet, which, in the middle of all this horror, struck Guy as rather poignant.

Fearing the imminent return of Aunt Alison, Roope quietly opened the door and hurried along the corridor to the stairs, avoiding any possible contact with people using the lift. As he left the block he noticed two people scurrying away towards a blue Mercedes Sport. In the warm glow of the morning light, for the first time terror clutched at his chest. He was beginning to understand what he had done. The red mist lifted. He raced to his car and wasted no time in setting off to join the family rendezvous in Pollença. He moved the rear view mirror to look at his face. It was harrowed and pale.

★★★★★

The road to Pollença was busy and Guy was keen to know whether he was being followed. He was in a procession of cars with no chance of overtaking on the hairpin bends, but as they snaked around the twisting road he saw the blue Mercedes Sport. Checking his rear view mirror he could only make out one figure, the driver. It was impossible to see him clearly, but instinctively Guy knew he wasn't on a joy ride. He slammed the accelerator, overtaking a coach at speed as it approached a blind bend. He held his nerve, swerving back into the lane as a farm vehicle in front of him braked. He managed to overtake it only to find himself behind another coach which was, in turn, stuck behind a group of cyclists. Glancing at the rear view again he saw both the blue Merc and a Ford Focus that had also been behind him all the way.

Unbeknown to Guy, the driver of the Merc, Diego, had been told by his partner, Osvaldo, to follow Guy Roope wherever he went. The pair had seen Roope enter the apartment block and leave some twenty minutes later.

Osvaldo had worked out that Davenport and Alison Galvin lived in the apartment block; he had been staking them out for days. He had a hunch the large, broad shouldered man who left the block had some connection with them. Whilst his partner trailed Roope, Osvaldo patiently waited, watching the apartment block from assorted sentry positions in the shopping mall. He, too, had seen Alison Galvin go out. Then he saw her again, but to his surprise, she didn't return to the apartment but instead turning left, ambling onto the quay. She passed one luxurious yacht after another, before approaching a speed boat that appeared to be waiting for her. Osvaldo checked his watch and seeing it was nearly eleven o'clock, followed her. A fine drizzle had set in, as he watched her hurry towards the boatman. Osvaldo panicked, fearing she was about to board the boat. If he lost her he would not be able to collect his money. He raced down the jetty and yelled, "You do not leave Mallorca, lady!"

Alison turned, frightened. Looking anxiously at her watch, she wondered where Don could have got to. He was never late.

"Look, I don't know who you are, but please leave me alone." Fearful, she pleaded with Carlos to help her onto the boat. Worse, she saw Osvaldo bend down, and start to clamber on to the bow of the boat behind her. Carlos protested.

"You are trespassing." Then he saw it. The thick tattoo of a serpent on his right forearm; he knew it belonged to a gang he had come across in the past and he had no desire to tangle with them again.

"I think you now lead me to your husband, lady." Osvaldo ordered. Alison knew she had no choice. She gripped the rail to hold her balance and stepped carefully across onto the pontoon. She glanced back at Carlos. He shrugged his shoulders as if to say "Sorry, but what can I do?"

Osvaldo accompanied Alison, in a slow, dignified walk back to the apartment block, looking to all the world as if he were her chaperone. He took her key, slowly turning it in the lock, before holding the door open for her to enter.

"Don, Don, dear." She called out hesitantly. Hearing no reply; she turned left towards their bedroom, imagining him doing some last minute packing. It was then that Alison saw the grey face of Don's corpse poking out above the duvet on the bed. She screamed and passed out.

Osvaldo was almost as startled as Alison and couldn't imagine how this had happened. He made for the door, callously abandoning Alison as she lay prostrate on the floor. He thought momentarily of kidnapping her but even he baulked at such a brutal action. Glancing behind him, he had a momentary flash of conscience. He returned to the bedroom and placed a pillow under the head of the stricken old lady; she began to stir.

"Where am I? Don dear, what's happening?" Rolling onto her side, slowly lifting herself up, she met her dead partner's face only inches from her own. Shrieking, she collapsed flat on the floor, blacking out again.

CHAPTER EIGHT

Justyn sat at the window, his head in his hands, deep in thought. The crack of a hunting gun high in the mountains pierced the morning air. Today was the day the two families were gathering to try to figure out, one last time, where Alison Galvin and Don Davenport might actually be. Everyone's morale was faltering and there was lots of talk about packing it in and going home. He couldn't make sense of events: Grant's fatal accident, Danny's dad's reincarnation, the attack on Davenport at Valldemossa. Why had Argentinian heavies tried to frighten him and Clare? To make matters worse he was becoming convinced that Grant's death wasn't an accident. Glancing up surreptitiously, watching Clare looking for something to wear, he was struggling to understand why she had behaved so oddly two afternoons ago. Where was she going when he saw her shoot out of the hotel car park?

"Put that frown away, JS, the wind may change!"

Before he could reply, a loud knocking on the door distracted them. Justyn jumped to his feet, pulled open the door and heaved a sigh of relief at the sight of Danny.

"Today's the day!" Danny breezed in. The other two looked doubtfully at him.

"Well whatever we decide, I'm staying on anyway. Oliver's arriving soon and I've got a hunch."

"Yes?"

"Quite simply, sooner or later we'll discover my mother and Davenport."

"Unlikely." Justyn's pessimistic mood persisted. "They've probably caught a fast boat to Ibiza by now."

"Maybe. But they'd have to come back. They've lived here for twenty years. They're too old now to up sticks again."

Justyn, wasn't convinced. Clare smiled warmly at Danny. She admired his resilience. Her phone buzzed.

"At … yeah, Okay, we'll do that, by twelve noon then, no worries." She turned to the others, "Mum's had a bit of a turn, wants us to meet up at Pollença at midday."

Danny nodded, picked up his phone, and rang Guy. No answer. He left him a voicemail, telling him of the change of venue. Justyn groaned in frustration, shifting in his chair. He desperately wanted time alone with Clare before the 'Aunty Summit'.

Having left the message, Danny remembered that he had seen Guy earlier.

"Oh by the way, you'll never guess who I spotted yesterday with a very pretty woman?"

"Who?" Justyn at that moment really couldn't care less.

"Guy!"

"What?" Clare was incredulous. "What did she look like?"

"Oh quite tall, thin, short dark hair. Really striking."

"Oh my God! That sounds like Leia. I had a coffee with her and she was telling me about this man she'd met whose name was Guy, but I didn't for one minute think it could be our Guy. She said he was sweet and gentle. She didn't actually mention what he looked like, otherwise I would have known straight away. Do you think I should say something?"

"Just stay out of it."

"But Leia said they were planning to get a boat to Ibiza."

"But he's supposed to be coming here. Perhaps it's not him after all."

"I think they were only going for twenty-four hours."

"Let's just see what happens."

"Well, I'll talk to Guy when I see him."

"Please yourself."

Danny didn't want to listen to any more bickering and quickly left the room. Justyn seized the moment to confront Clare about what she'd been up to. Slipping out of her negligée, she misinterpreted his mood.

"Don't even think about it."

"I'm not, don't worry. I'm not myself at the moment."

Clare continued dressing. After more than twenty years of prevarication she knew just how contrary Justyn could be.

"One question?"

"Yes?" she pursed her lips, unsure she would like what was coming.

"Do you think Grant's death really was an accident?"

"Anywhere other than here or the Almalfi Coast I would be more suspicious, but I know the danger on these roads. I'll never forget the coastal route from here to Pollença."

"Guess so."

★★★★★

As twelve noon approached, the elderly sisters shuffled up and down the terrace. They were both agitated and unable to keep still. The air was oppressive and humid. Pat kept saying storm clouds would soon gather but her sister wasn't sure whether she meant it metaphorically. Despite being in Mallorca for five days, they had hardly seen their respective offspring. Pat had been visited only once by Clare and

Horace, on separate occasions, and Diana also only once by her son, Guy. Their plan to find and confront their sister, Alison, hadn't really got going. Reluctant to confront Danny, they were uneasy at Justyn Silver phoning them. Was he leading the search? Diana was continually patrolling up and down the patio, taking the steps down to the pool and then back again to the outside terrace, muttering how life never went the way it should. Pat was more agile and kept herself busy by sorting things out: unloading and loading the dishwasher, taking out the rubbish and brushing the floors. She was respectful of the villa her friends had let them borrow and couldn't stop cleaning surfaces and putting things away.

On the dot of twelve the buzzer on the garden gates sounded. Pat picked up the kitchen phone and saw on the screen Danny, her own children, Horace and Clare and Clare's boyfriend, Justyn, waiting outside the gates. She saw no sign of Diana's son, Guy.

"Where's Guy?" Diana shrilled, watching them file in through the kitchen door.

"No idea," Danny replied. Pat and Diana exchanged glances.

"Don't worry," Justyn intervened, "Danny's on our side. Don't visit the sins of the parents on the children. He's had the worse time of all." Extending a supportive arm around Danny's shoulders, he led him through.

"Where is he? Where's Guy? Where is he?" Diana's frenetic questioning grated on the others, particularly Justyn. On the table his fingers tapped out the rhythm of the Chas & Dave's song, 'rabbit, rabbit, rabbit, rabbit, rabbit' singing in his head, 'why don't you give it a rest, you're becoming a pest'. He couldn't hold back a giggle.

"I'm sorry, Diana, but you haven't stopped going on about Guy since we arrived." Diana glared at him.

"You Okay, Clare?" She didn't look at all well.

"I bet Guy's gone to Ibiza and forgotten all about the meeting."

"Well if Guy can go clubbing all night long in Ibiza, all power to his elbow." Justyn winced at idiot Horace's favourite expression. He had used it constantly since he'd arrived on the island. He struggled to resist the urge to flatten Horace with his own elbow.

The conversation was desultory. They were no nearer to finding Alison and Don and had no idea who had attacked Davenport in Valldemossa or who was driving the car on the road back from Pollença. In short they had drawn blanks all round and Justyn was feeling frustrated.

Clare stood up, lifting a hand to refuse Justyn's assistance and only just made it to the lavatory where she retched over and over again. Justyn was quickly by her side holding her steady.

"That was a bit of a turn, is it food poisoning, do you think?"

Clare stood up and struggled to clear her throat,

"Don't think so – I'm scared, JS, I'm really scared for Leia."

"Why?"

"Guy's got a dangerous side. He's always had a terrible temper. He's not a very nice man when you get to know him. Not a nice man at all. You know he killed people when he was in the SAS. Apparently got quite a kick out of it; Mum heard all about it from Diana. He used to boast about it. We also heard his leaving the SAS wasn't exactly his decision. And he's even worse when he drinks."

"Well, he would have had to kill people in the SAS wouldn't he? But surely he wouldn't harm Leia? I mean, why would he? It sounds as if he's besotted with her?"

Clare continued, "He disrespects women, JS, thinks they're only good for one thing."

"I think you should lie down for a bit." He took her by the hand and led her into a spare bedroom. Soon Danny was knocking on the door. Justyn tried to get rid of him. He really wanted Clare to have a rest.

"Sorry Dan, need to back off. Clare's had a bit of a turn, she's worried about Leia being with Guy."

"Why?"

"He's dangerous, Danny. We've all underestimated him, his past, his difficult life."

"Jesus Christ, Justyn, we've all had difficult lives, why the sudden concern about Guy now?"

"Well, where is he? He should be here by now."

Before Danny could answer, the buzzer went at the front gate.

Diana checked the entry camera and shrieked.

"It's Guy!" Guy walked in ignoring his mother as she rushed to embrace him.

"You old whore!" he spat, deliberately avoiding eye contact.

"Guy, darling, what are you saying?" Her voice faltering, Diana stumbled and fell backwards into a chair.

"You old whore!" he repeated, more venomously. "I knew you took lovers. I never knew you did it before I was born! So that's why and how I'm here! No wonder the man I thought was Dad was so cold." Diana, at first speechless, took a deep, uneven breath.

"No, no, now listen, there's so much you don't know." Her voice was pleading. She rose again from her chair, only to stagger and lose balance. Pat rushed to support her, but lacked the strength, leaving Danny to hurry forward and wrap his right arm around Diana's waist, as she swayed on her feet. Hearing the raised voices, Justyn shot out of Clare's bedroom, in time to hear Pat ask: "What are you saying, Guy? What exactly are you accusing your mother of?"

"Infidelity. Being a slut. Sleeping with the enemy!"

"What enemy are you talking about?" Danny fired back.

Fixing a stare on his mother, Guy shouted, "She knows!" His wild eyes scanned the room. No one doubted he was capable of doing something extreme.

"Okay Guy," Diana croaked, struggling to get a grip, "I won't deny it, Donald was your biological father, but I thought I was in love at the time."

"In love!" hollered Guy, "With him! That vile specimen of human flesh. With him?"

"Look, Guy," Justyn's measured tone intervened, "just who the hell are you talking about?"

"Don Davenport!" Diana lurched forward, Danny caught her just in time.

Danny stared hard at Roope and asked, "How did you find out?" Justyn saw fear on Guy's face. The old soldier was covering something up. His swagger was draining away.

"You'd better tell us where Davenport is."

"Illness does its early work in secret." Justyn couldn't recall where or when he'd read this, but it came into his head as he watched Guy. He was breathing too quickly and looked sick. Discovering Davenport was his biological father had taken its toll. Wrapping his arm around Guy's shoulder, Justyn led him firmly out to the patio where the table had been set for their meeting; Pat was clearing away coffee cups. They sat down at the table next to Danny.

"I'll bring some fresh," Pat offered, trying to sound more breezy than she felt.

"So Guy, what's going on?"

"What do you mean, Justyn, what's going on?"

"How did you find out about Davenport?" Danny interrupted, glancing down at Roope's shaking hands.

"I don't have to answer to either of you, hippy boy," and then turning to Danny "or you, ginger …"

"It's a perfectly reasonable question." Danny wasn't put off by his aggression.

Justyn felt agitated and got up from the table. He couldn't stand

Roope and had a feeling something terrible had happened. He imagined how police interrogators must feel when they know they have brought in the right suspect, only to meet a brick wall. Roope broke the silence:

"Where's Leia?"

Justyn ignored the question. "Did you have Davenport duffed up in Valldemossa?" He didn't necessarily think he had, but he was trying it on.

Guy's forehead creased. "How much more of this shit do I have to take? Of course I didn't."

The buzzer from the gate pinged again. Clare emerged from her bedroom on the left of the kitchen, and checked the security monitor. There was a *policía* standing at the gates. She didn't want to share this information with the others, so went up to Justyn and whispered in his ear. Holding back, deliberately showing no reaction to what he'd just heard, Justyn stared at Roope. Were the *policías* here because of him? Clare returned to press the entry button. Three *policías* stormed up through the garden onto the patio. Guy flew out of his chair, but the *policías* pounced on him. One grabbed him in an armlock, the other shackled him in handcuffs.

"We are arresting you ... " Before they finished the formalities, Clare gasped. She was standing by the monitor.

"What?" Justyn yelled, jumping to his feet, rushing to join her.

"Oh my God! It's Scarface, one of the Argentinian thugs. Hang on, someone's running to join him!" she shrieked. The *policías*, who were still outside, ignored her, trying to contain Roope who was struggling violently. Inside, a third *policía* explained that they had received a call from Puerto Portals alerting them to the murder of Davenport, followed by an anonymous tip-off, giving a very clear lead as to who was responsible. They hadn't yet traced the caller but having found Davenport's dead body in the apartment, were convinced that it was true. The entry door had been left wide open and Alison Galvin was nowhere to be seen.

The two *policías* were still finding it hard to overpower Roope. The fine drizzle that had begun a little earlier was now turning into heavy rain, making the patio slippery and dangerous. Surprising them with his strength, he wrestled free of their grip, roundhouse kickboxing one, then the other, despite having his hands cuffed in front of him. The officers shouted back to their colleague who was still in the villa.

Roope ran as fast as his shackled state would allow towards the gate, only to be confronted by Diego, who had now been joined by his partner Osvaldo, coming up the drive. Roope swerved to his right to avoid the chasing *policías* but was floored by a single punch from Diego. The two *policías*, joined by the third, made no mistake this time, hauling him towards their car, slapping him hard for good measure. As he looked back over his shoulder, Guy saw his mother's pitiful face at a window. He knew he had finally broken her heart.

Osvaldo and Diego swaggered into the villa, brushing past Clare who was clearing up the kitchen. Diana could be heard from a downstairs bedroom moaning loudly and becoming delirious. Pat, distraught at her sister's state, rushed up the stairs shrieking at the others, to "call an ambulance *now*!" Clare picked up the phone from her work top and dialled the emergency services. Then she thought better of it. Her aunt was hysterical rather than ill and there seemed little point in adding another crisis to a situation that was already spiralling out of control.

By now everyone, except Diana had moved into the sitting room of the villa. The rain was still pouring down outside and there was a strange atmosphere of shock, suspicion and anticipation. No one spoke. The silence was broken by Osvaldo. He stood at the door.

"We want the money."

Justyn was bemused. What money? His jaw dropped, however,

when the Argentinians went over to Danny, who pulled a huge wad of notes from his pocket. Justyn was dumbfounded.

"I'm sorry," Danny began, "I couldn't tell you, Justyn, it was too raw, too difficult ... I had to find Mum and Davenport. When I found Dad I thought of asking them to stand down, but it doesn't work that way; besides I still needed to find Mum. I've really hated hiding this from you, Justyn and well, from all of you."

"If you sup with the devil ..." Justyn tapped his fingers on the table.

"Don't be too quick to judge him, JS ..." Clare's soft voice cut in. "You see I tried to hire them as well, but Danny, it turns out, had got there first." Justyn shot her a glance that gave nothing away, neither condemning nor approving. He hoped this would be the catalyst for Clare to come clean with him, but he also feared it might break their relationship once and for all.

"And you, Horace, did you try and hire them as well? It seems I'm the one behind the eight ball here!" He half-smiled, feeling more foolish than angry.

"No, I've not been involved with it," Justyn nodded, thinking this more than likely, knowing Horace as he did.

"I'm sorry I didn't tell you before, JS." Clare looked at him plaintively, hoping her own clumsy attempt to hire hitmen wouldn't cause another speed bump in their relationship.

Danny sat down and counted out the pay off for Diego and Osvaldo. They had tracked Alison and Davenport to Puerto Portals so they had earned their reward.

Clare turned to Osvaldo, "Why did you try to harm us?"

"We had to scare you off – you knew us – we sorry." Osvaldo shrugged, motioning to Diego, leading him out of the kitchen door. They didn't stick around to find out if Clare accepted their apology.

"So, how much did that little escapade set you back?" Justyn asked.

"About fifteen grand."

"Good grief!" Danny didn't bother to reply, knowing now that thanks to this whole adventure he was most likely to share some thirty million pounds with his sister. He smiled weakly at Justyn, looking a little sheepish.

They all went back to staring into space, trying to understand what they had started and where it was all going to end.

Pat broke the silence by suggesting she make a nice cup of tea for everyone. Bizarrely it seemed like a very good idea. While they listened to the reassuring sounds of cups and saucers being assembled, Clare's thoughts turned to Leia.

"I'm still worried about Leia. I should have warned her properly about Roope. She's such a nice, sweet girl and she's already had so much to deal with. I feel we've really let her down."

"Where could she be?"

"Shall we call the police?"

"It's too late to ask Roope, he'll be locked up by now. They won't risk him slipping them again."

"One thing that's really important." said Justyn, "who tipped them off? Was it one of us?"

"What?"

"I mean, we know why the Argentinians were here," Justyn sounded anxious, "but how did the police know Roope was here? Who tipped them off? Was it one of us?"

"No" they said in unison, their attention taken by yet another ping from the outside gate. No one moved.

Pat paused in her tea making and inspected the monitor in the kitchen.

"There's a young lady out there. I've no idea who she is." Justyn joined her to see the lady in question grind out a cigarette as she waited anxiously to be let in. Clare went into the kitchen to have a look.

"Oh my God! It's Leia."

Clare rushed out of the villa, greeting the new arrival with a warm hug, before standing back anxiously to take stock of Leia's face. "You're Okay, aren't you?"

"Yes, thanks, don't worry." Clare threaded her arm through Leia's and escorted her into the villa. Leia looked relieved to be with them and, now that the rain had stopped, she took the seat at the table on the terrace, so recently vacated by her lover. They all waited politely for her to speak.

Swallowing hard, she cleared her throat, "I followed Guy here. In fact I've watched him for the best part of twenty four hours. I saw the police go in. Have they got him, properly got him?" Clare nodded. The others watched her. They knew she was Guy's latest conquest. "I think he's done something very bad. We were in Puerto Portals, heading to Ibiza on my friend Carlos's boat." Leia paused, dabbing her eyes with a tissue.

"There was this old couple," she fixed her eyes straight ahead, concentrating on what had happened, "and when he saw them talking to Carlos, he didn't want me, he didn't want me anywhere near."

"What old couple?" Danny became agitated. Leia started to describe them.

Danny didn't wait to hear anymore. He jumped up, tore through the kitchen, and out of the door. Justyn ran after him.

"Where you heading?"

"Police Station, Puerto Portals."

Justyn returned to the others on the terrace, raising his eyes to the sky. Leia stared ahead. They sat in silence.

"One thing, Leia," Justyn broke the tension, "do you know who called the police?"

"Yes."

"And?"

"Me!" She blushed, her voice sounded different, cold. "You see, I knew Guy was up to something. One moment he was all over me, the next it was like – 'get lost!' I thought he planned to take the boat by himself to Ibiza. He heard the old couple say they would be back at eleven the next day so I thought Guy must be planning to go on the same trip. He claimed he didn't know them. I became obsessed with finding out what was going on. He thought I'd gone back to Deià. He told me to take the car. But I went to stay with my friend, Isabella. She lives near the marina. This morning I went back to where I'd left Guy. I waited out of sight, careful that he never saw me. I saw him enter this apartment block. He re-appeared about ten minutes later, he looked as if he'd been in a fight. I was so angry with him, I decided to call the police. I was afraid that he might hurt me if he saw me, I've had trouble with a violent man before. I was also afraid he had hurt the old couple. I then decided to follow him. When I got here I just knew he'd done something very bad. I didn't dare come in so have been waiting outside until the police took him away. Did the police say anything?"

"You're a brave girl," Clare tried to reassure her. The others looked alarmed.

CHAPTER NINE

The officer behind the reception desk at the *Policia Local de Puerto Portals* was a large, thick-set man with a shock of black hair and eyebrows and moustache to match. He watched Danny as he approached the desk. He was the kind of imposing policeman who made you feel guilty just to be there. Danny realised that he was going to have to calm his nerves and use all his charm and rudimentary Spanish to get this man on his side.

"Mi madre."

The officer remained impassive.

"Tu madre?"

"Si, mi madre. En peligro."

"Papeles."

Papers? Danny didn't quite understand, but then the penny dropped and he realised the man wanted ID.

Relieved to find his passport in his back pocket, Danny passed it across the counter. The *policía* thumbed through it and, without speaking or looking up, took it into a private office, closing the door behind him. Danny heard excited voices coming from the room. A petite, middle-aged policewoman then appeared, beckoning with an elaborate flick of her hand, for him to come to her office. Danny followed her and took a seat. Fearing bad news, swallowing hard, he prepared himself for the worst. The officer held Danny's gaze, drew breath and broke the awkward silence.

"Your mother is in danger?" Danny was relieved that she spoke English. "We do not know at this time where she is, but we have no reason to suspect she is not alive. Her partner, however, has been found dead in an apartment here in Puerto Portals. We believe the apartment he shared with your mother." She watched Danny carefully as she spoke, keen to monitor his reaction.

"How? I mean, what happened to him?" Danny struggled to speak, feeling as though the air was being sucked out of the room.

"He was strangled, we believe there was a struggle with an intruder."

There was a knock on the door. The broad-shouldered officer he'd spoken to at reception reappeared, talking animatedly to his colleague in Spanish, before leading her out into the corridor. Danny cursed in frustration, unable to understand a word they were saying. His phone bleeped. It was Martin Whitlock. He let it go to voicemail: the call could wait. Almost immediately the officers reappeared. The female spoke first.

"We've just received news. Mrs Galvin, er, your mother, has been spotted on a CCTV camera in a shopping mall here in Puerto Portals, at 11.20 a.m. yesterday. We believe this was very soon after she found Mr Davenport's body in their apartment."

Rising to his feet, Danny yelled, "Where is she now?"

"Come this way, please, we can show you the CCTV footage." Led across to an adjacent room, he tried to control his breathing, preparing himself for the footage. His mother was in an alleyway at the shopping mall. Wearing a trademark, very old Mary Quant raincoat, buttoned to the neck in her usual way, her head was shrouded in a Hermès scarf, but she could be clearly seen engaging in conversation with a much younger looking woman, with blonde hair. They appeared to know each other. After no more than thirty seconds' discussion they were walking away together. Knowing she'd just discovered her partner's murdered body, he was surprised to see his mother looking neither anxious nor distraught. He saw her face clearly. They could have been a mother and daughter meeting up for a shopping trip. He could only just make out from the footage the two leaving the mall and getting into what appeared to be a waiting car.

"Do you know the younger woman here?" Danny asked for the footage to be played again. The second viewing jogged his memory. He asked to see it once more. "Is it a family member? Do you have a sister, Mr Galvin?"

"Yes I do, I do have a sister," he replied in a dull robotic voice, still distracted and asking to view the footage one more time.

"Is it her?"

"No." The officers looked at each other; it would have been very helpful if it had been. "No, it's not," Danny elaborated, "but I think I can tell you who she is." The officers waited, expectantly. "It's Monika."

"Who's Monika?"

"My father's companion."

"We must speak to your father right now, then we might find your mother."

"I don't think so … "

"What? Why not?"

"He had a massive heart attack and died in Deià last week." Danny fought back the thought that his mother might have been involved in some way in Davenport's murder. Why and how could she appear so relaxed in the video, given her gruesome discovery?

The *policías* assured Danny they could track the car but would need a little time. He was ushered into yet another room, offered coffee, and asked to wait. His phone rang.

"Er, hello, is that Danny?" a frail and elderly voice enquired.

Danny immediately recognised it, not quite daring to believe whom he thought it belonged to.

"Yes, yes, who's this?"

"Your Mum, darling." Danny squeezed the mobile hard in his hand.

"Well, well, at least you're alive," he gasped, "are you Okay? I'm at the police station and everyone's looking for you." His mother paused, he heard her take a breath;

"Look, darling, I know this might sound strange," more hesitation, "but you mustn't contest your father's will." He assumed she meant the old will. He felt a return of the old dizziness; there was so much he wanted to say but he knew he had to be calm and keep the conversation going.

"I'm going to ignore that remark, Mum. I'd like to see you, it's been a long time." Danny was afraid she might hang up. "Look, Mum, let's meet, please."

"Um, darling, I'm told that's not possible …" The line went dead.

Danny repeated aloud "I'm told that's not possible." What was going on? Had she been kidnapped? He charged out of the room. The station seemed deserted. He was in a corridor with closed doors on each side. He decided to knock on a door at random and was fortunate that the English speaking officer was sitting behind a desk. He explained what had happened and she took his phone and asked him to go back to the waiting room. Within minutes she was back, returning the phone without further comment. He noticed two missed calls, and two voicemails. One was from Martin Whitlock, one from Justyn. He played them in order.

"Danny, I've good news for you. We've got Counsel's advice. I won't say too much now, please call me as soon as you can."

"Hi Dan, please call urgently." Knowing Justyn didn't usually over dramatise, he returned this call first.

"Hi, what's up?"

"It's Diana, your Aunt Diana, she's in a coma." Somehow he knew what was coming.

"Has she tried to kill herself?"

"Yes. She took a massive overdose of sleeping pills. It happened when Pat left her alone when Leia arrived."

"What's the prognosis?" Justyn didn't answer.

"Just a moment, Dan." Seconds later Justyn resumed the conversation. "The hospital's been on," he paused, "I'm sorry, but Diana's passed away."

Danny sighed, recalling the awful scene with Guy.

"How tragic, how unbelievably tragic …" Both fell silent for a while, as if observing an official silence. Thoughts of Diana raced through Danny's mind; how she had doted on Guy, how her whole life had revolved around him and how in the end he had destroyed her. Justyn broke the silence.

"Where are you Danny?"

"Still at the police station. Davenport's been found murdered, but they have some CCTV footage of Mum being led away by someone in the local shopping mall."

"Oh Christ, do you know who by?"

"Yes, yes I do."

"And … "

"It's Monika," before Justyn could ask, Danny explained. She's the woman who was Dad's companion. I've no idea how long they were together. She's the woman I found living with him at his villa."

"Uh huh." There was a pause.

"You Okay, Dan?" Danny's attention was taken again by the figures of the 'little and large' police combination, entering his waiting room.

"Yeah fine, thanks. Can't talk now. Speak later."

"Tenemos algo." The large male officer spoke first. Then his smaller colleague continued, "We have tracked the car, a grey-coloured Citröen, we think it belongs to Eastern Europeans, probably members of a gang." The colour drained from Danny's face.

"And what happens now?"

"We have a tracker car following it. I'm afraid your mother may have been kidnapped. If so you will probably receive a demand for money very soon. We don't know how she knew this woman. It seems she left her apartment and wandered down to the mall, where the woman was waiting for her."

"I see."

"Can we ask: does your mother have money?"

"Yes, you could say that."

"It would help us if you can give us an idea of how much she might be worth, so we can have some idea of the sum they might want. Sorry to be so personal." The female officer's eyes drilled into Danny.

"You can, I don't mind telling you. We all want her release as soon as possible. I believe she inherited a sizeable share of one hundred million pounds!" Danny waited for the reaction. The two officers stared at him in silence.

"Do you mind if I stay here to catch up on some phone calls?" The two *policías* exchanged glances, then nodded. Danny concealed his real reason for delaying, which was that he was hoping to hear news of Roope. There was little he could do to track down his mother, it was much better to leave that to the police. He needed to try to see Roope. He might well know what had happened to her.

"Just one more thing. Do you mind if I ask who stands to inherit the money?" The officer surprised Danny with her bluntness.

"You can ask, but I have no idea." She blinked at the reply, not believing a word of it.

"You may need protection, Mr Galvin. We can help with this." The officer had jumped to her own conclusions.

"Thanks, I'm really very grateful, but shall we just see how things play out?" The officers left the room, but the female turned to look back at Danny, just before closing the door. She was thinking that she might just be looking at someone soon to be the wealthiest person she had ever met.

Danny returned Martin Whitlock's call.

"I thought I'd be hearing from you. We've got Counsel's Advice, can you come in for a meeting?"

"Uh, no, not at present, er, Martin, it's all a bit complicated but I will soon. Can you tell me the gist of it?"

"Well, as expected Chambers think the new will is entirely lawful and that your father, Paul Galvin, was in sound mind when it was drawn up. I've requested a mental capacity test from your father's doctor, I had his details on file. It should confirm your father was in sound mind. It's entirely coincidental that he had a heart attack the very next day. Davenport, it would appear, doesn't have a leg to stand on."

"He doesn't."

"What?"

"He doesn't have a leg to stand on," pausing, clearing his throat, "because he's dead. Davenport's dead."

Whitlock stared at the phone. "When and how did that happen?"

"He was found murdered yesterday." Danny paused, giving Whitlock a chance to absorb the information.

"How terrible, do you know how or why. Who found him?"

"Few details yet, Martin, but they've made an arrest."

"Who?" Whitlock paced around his office.

"Guy Roope, my cousin." Martin Whitlock, used to his clients' affairs unfolding at a rather more sedate pace, slumped backwards on to a sofa. Stretching out his legs, he closed his eyes, recapping. "Now let me get this clear. Davenport manipulated your grandfather's estate, swindling your two aunts; then he and your mother deceived you and your sister into thinking your father was dead, now Davenport's discovered murdered. And the prime suspect is your cousin, Guy Roope, who happens to arrive on the island at the same time as all the aggrieved parties?" Whitlock exhaled loudly, waiting for Danny's confirmation.

"True, but only one of the group, Guy Roope, has been arrested on suspicion of murder. They've got him in custody."

Danny's attention was taken by shouting from the corridor, followed by an alarm bell and seconds later, police sirens, blaring from the car park. "Martin, I'll call you back." He rushed out of the waiting room and rattled the office door but it was locked. He called out, but his shouts were ignored. All he could hear was the sound of running feet and car and motor bike engines starting up outside. Finally he caught an officer's attention.

"Qué ha pasado?"

It was easy to understand the reply;

"Un prisionero escapó."

"Como se llama?" The officer, looking down, squinted at a piece of paper in his hand. Danny said the name for him. "Guy Roope."

"Si, señor."

★★★★★

"Clare, it's Danny. Is Leia still with you?" the words rushed out.

"She stayed overnight but left at about 7 a.m., saying she needed to get to the shop in Deià."

"Why?"

"Roope's escaped!" Danny's voice had become curiously high

pitched in his panic.

Clare was silent. She couldn't believe what she was hearing.

"Hello, are you there … Clare?"

"How could it happen? Are you sure?" Clare recovered, "Didn't the police have him?"

"Yes, he was being held in the cells at Puerto Portals police station. I'm there now."

"Oh my God!" Staring across at Justyn, she held her hand over the phone, and repeated what she was hearing.

Danny rang off and Clare shared the news with the others in the villa. There was general disbelief that Guy could have escaped, concern at what he might do next and a stunned inability to make sense of what was happening.

Justyn suggested that the least they could do was to try and find Leia and make sure she was safe. Clare wasn't sure, and although she was worried about Leia, she thought the best thing would be for everyone to stay put until the police gave them some news.

Tired of sitting around, Justyn grabbed his jacket and pecked Clare on the cheek. "I'm going to take the bike and visit Leia at that shop she said she works in."

Clare knew she couldn't stop him.

"Good luck. Keep in touch."

They heard the loud engine of the Harley-Davidson as it raced down the road.

"What a kid!" muttered Horace.

★★★★★

Leia arrived early at the village store and, as always, locked herself in after going through the back entrance. She started to tidy the shelves, knowing that a delivery would arrive in about an hour's time. Unusually for that time of day, she heard the ring of the front door bell. As she approached she saw, through the smoked glass in the upper half of the door, the silhouette of a man. Keeping the security chain in place and tentatively opening the door, she recognised the silhouette's owner: Guy Roope.

"Let me in." He didn't request, he commanded and wedged his foot in the door. Leia considered using the alarm button by the door but then remembered it was broken.

"Look honey, I'm really sorry about what happened in Puerto Portals. I'll never ask you to leave again." His voice pleaded, she hesitated. Leia noticed his sweating forehead and saw his right wrist was swathed in a bandage and in spite of everything, she couldn't quite bring herself to turn him away and she knew he would force his way in whatever she did. She dreaded to think what he would do if he knew she had betrayed him. "Please darling, let me in." His voice lower, softer, reduced her fear; reluctantly, against her own better judgement, she slowly released the security chain. He withdrew his foot and the door edged open. She gasped when she saw what a terrible state he was in. His face was bruised and puffy, his eyes were bloodshot and there was a wildness about him that was terrifying. He grabbed her and held her so tightly she felt every bone in her body might break.

"I've missed you." He sounded caring, tender, before suddenly demanding, "What time does this place open?"

"In about an hour."

"Now, listen to me and everything will be fine. But if you double cross me …" he paused, looking intently into her eyes for clues of whether she had already. "I need to speak to my mother. I was vile to her yesterday. I really regret it." He saw some of Leia's warmth returning. "I'm not a good person, Leia, you shouldn't have got mixed up with me, you're just a child." His eyes were moistening.

Sensing the real danger had passed, she put a hand on his arm. She felt ashamed, that this man, a fugitive, most likely a murderer, could still excite her. The strangest thought entered her head. She had read about women writing letters of undying love to serial killers on death row. Was she in the grip of a similar fascination?

He leant forward, kissing her gently on the lips. She responded, slowly kissing him, then releasing more force and passion than she had ever done before.

"Let's escape, Leia, go to South America, we'll change names, identities."

She stared back, daring herself to agree to go with him. They were so absorbed with one another that neither of them heard a noise outside. Justyn had left his motorbike a short distance from the shop and was now outside the door. He called Leia's mobile. Guy answered.

"Yes?"

"Oh, hi Guy, where are you? Have you given 'Old Bill' the slip?" He realised that he sounded ridiculous, pretending to be breezy and jocular and not fooling anyone.

"Yes, a little bit of local difficulty, but have been released now, no worries," he paused, "bit worried about my Mum, though. I need to call her, d'you know if she's still in Pollença?"

Justyn cleared his throat, "I'm sorry Guy. I need see you. There's something I need to tell you in person."

"Well that's not possible right now. What's happened?"

"I've got some bad news for you," Justyn hesitated, "your mother passed away earlier this morning."

"Are you playing some kind of game?" Guy snarled.

"I'm afraid to say that she took her own life."

Guy, the ex SAS officer, now on the run from a murder charge, buried his face in his hands and howled. He crumpled to the floor.

Justyn didn't need his phone to hear him, but knew he needed to get into the shop very quickly.

"Oh God. I was so unkind to my Mum, Leia, so brutal. Now she's dead. She loved me so much." Leia leant down, putting her hands on his shoulders. "I've done a bad thing, Leia, a terrible thing. I need to hide, Leia, I haven't got long … d'you know anyone who might take me in, might help me?" His dreams of them escaping together were fading; his only chance now was to make a run for it on his own. He silently resolved to return for her one day.

Sympathy for this damaged, dangerous man who had so briefly illuminated her life, overcame Leia's fear. Having reported him to the police, she now wanted to help him to escape. Perhaps one day she would be able to make sense of it.

She pulled her address book from her bag and flicked through the pages.

"Andrzej … Andrzej is your man. He's Polish I think. He works with the gangs, mainly Romanians." She ripped a page out of her book. "This is his address and number, but you'll need to pay him. Don't ask how I know him." She didn't have the chance to ask him not to mention her to Andrzej.

"Is there any cash here?"

"In the safe."

"Can you open it?"

"Yes. I know the combination." She felt bad stealing from the people who had been so kind to her but she had decided on a path and there was no other way.

The lock on the safe made a reassuring click as the lock opened. Guy pulled open the door and grabbed the bundles of Euros, held together with rubber bands. He stuffed them into his pockets and then turned round to face her. He took her face in his hands.

"I'm truly sorry for what I have to do now." Leia felt a wave of fear. She saw him take a knife from the drawer at the counter. Had she made a fatal mistake? Would he now kill her?

"Please Guy, please." A loud banging at the back door interrupted Roope. He turned to see a large shadow looming on the other side of the glass.

"Tell them you'll open the door in a minute, say you're in the loo." She did as she was told. Roope hurriedly bound and gagged her, before tying her very tightly to a chair.

In a split second he'd unlocked the front door, rushed out, and using the key Justyn had absentmindedly left in the ignition, fired up the Harley-Davidson and sped off. Meanwhile, Justyn found a heavy steel pole that had been discarded outside the back door and used it to splinter the lock. Once inside he untied Leia as fast as he could. Roope had not held back on the tightness of the ligatures. He had gagged her and her cheeks were turning purple.

"Roope?" Leia nodded. She tried to stand before collapsing into his arms.

CHAPTER TEN

Danny paced up and down the corridor; he'd slept poorly. He had returned to the police station desperate to hear news of his mother. He knew he needed to call his sister, Sharon but was slightly dreading it.

For many years Sharon had lived an alternative existence. She had been a punk in the seventies, a 'Goth' in the eighties and had pretty much cut herself off from her family. He remembered her living in a commune in Whitby and everyone from her past who tried to contact her had been rebuffed. Perversely, every year she always turned up at Chelmsford railway station on Christmas Eve, asking to be picked up. Once home, she would then proceed to shower the family with peculiar gifts – handmade angels and an unusual take on scenes from the 'Birth at Bethlehem'. Come Boxing Day she would summon Danny to drive her back to the station disappearing again from their lives. It changed in the mid nineties when Danny told her that their father had died and their mother had gone to Mallorca with Don Davenport. The news shook her back into the real world. She cut her hair short, re-trained as a dental nurse and from then on, commuted every day to Harley Street to a private dental practice. Danny had finally grown closer to her but never felt he really knew her.

"Hi Sharon, how's things?" He straightened in his chair.

"Okay really, apart from the trains. Liverpool Street tonight was sheer chaos." Danny relaxed a little and smiled at the way his sister had become yet another frustrated commuter.

"Can we talk? Where are you?"

"Sure. I'm at home."

"Well, I need to tell you what's been going on here in Mallorca."

"I didn't know you were even there."

"No. I should have told you. But I had no idea what, if anything, was going to happen."

"Okay."

"Well, here goes. I found Dad alive but he's now dead. Davenport got tracked down but is now dead and Mum's been kidnapped. We've been searching for her. Her sisters, well one of them now, and our cousins, are all here."

"Have you been drinking?"

"I wish I had, but it's all true and Guy Roope, has been arrested for the murder of Don."

"And I'm off to Mars tomorrow, then a tour of the Milky Way!"

"Sharon, I know this all sounds ridiculous, but you have to believe me, you really have to! Dad never died back in '96. You were in Whitby. I was on Mykonos. His death was faked. Nobody I know ever saw his corpse."

"What? Who faked it?" She was beginning to believe him.

"Well, Mum and Davenport, primarily, but Dad played along. You have to believe me when I tell you I know Dad loved us both very much."

"Why should I believe that? If he's been alive all these years and never contacted me, it's a very strange way of showing it!"

"Would thirty million pounds do it?

"How much?"

"I think you heard!

"It turns out that our grandfather was blackmailed into fixing his will by Mum and Davenport."

"But what about Dad?"

"Well, I guess he wasn't blameless." Sharon fell silent.

"Are you still there? Can you hear me?" Danny saw she was no longer on the line; a moment later she called him back.

"I'm sorry, I had to sit down. I'm Okay now. It's difficult to take all this in."

"No I'm the one who's sorry, so sorry. I should have flown back, told you face to face, it's just I can't while I'm trying to find Mum."

"I understand. I think I'd better fly out. Give me the details of where you are. I'll join you as soon as I can get a flight. I want to find Mum too."

"Great, that's really great news, Shar!"

"Text or email me with all the details of where everyone is."

"Yeah, sure. Justyn Silver's here with Clare, staying at the same hotel as me – they're back together by the way."

"Are the aunts with you as well?"

"Well, not exactly,"

"What do you mean, not exactly?"

"Do you want more bad news?"

"Can things get any worse?"

"Pat and Diana have been staying at a villa in Pollença. Pat's moving to our hotel today, but poor old Diana died yesterday."

"Fucking hell! How did she die?"

"She killed herself."

The line went dead again and stayed dead.

★★★★★

Clare cast an anxious glance over her shoulder as she hurried down the street from her car to the shop in Deià. She arrived minutes after Justyn had rescued Leia.

"He's nicked my bike!" Justyn greeted her. "I've told the police. They're on his tail already."

"Not *your* bike strictly speaking, JS. Only a machine. How's Leia?" She breezed past him, spotting Leia sitting on a plastic chair outside, her head bowed; Clare bent down to cradle her in her arms, almost folding her into her.

"You poor darling, don't speak. The police will get him." Leia moved her lips but no words came out.

"She's had a really bad time, I found her bound and gagged."

"For how long?"

"Not long."

"Where's Danny?"

"Not sure. I'll call him." Before he could, Danny called him.

"Yeah, hi, where are you?"

"I came back to the police station. We think Mum's been kidnapped. They're tracking the car she's in, with, would you believe, Monika? Before Justyn could reply he continued: "I've told Sharon everything. She's on her way now. How's Aunt Pat?"

"Well, Clare's here with me here in Deià, and Horace is bringing their mother down to our hotel this afternoon. But Danny, there's something else."

"What?"

"After you phoned to say Roope had escaped."

Danny cut him short, "You should have seen the commotion. Roope blitzed his way out."

"Yeah, well then he blitzed his way into Leia's shop!"

"You're kidding!" .

"No I'm not. But it's all Okay now. Well at least *she* is, Roope's gone on the run with my bike! ... well, my hired bike." Danny, despite, or possibly because of the tension of the situation, giggled. "Don't laugh!"

"I'm sorry JS, but it's a bit ironic!"

"Yeah, sure, but he nearly killed Leia, She could barely breathe. The bastard had gagged her so tightly."

"Thank God you got there, mate. Where's she now?"

"Clare's with her. We're just waiting for the Melias to arrive, then we're taking her to our hotel. Managed to get her a room. Anyway, how long before you can join us back here?"

"I'm going to give it until noon. I'll hook up with you all after that."

"We could keep an eye on your father's villa."

"Thanks, that could be helpful."

"By the way, why do you think Monika's involved?"

"Well money, probably. I guess she was excluded from the will!"

"How do you know?"

"The lawyer handling Dad's estate told me she's outraged that Dad changed his will the day before he died. Dad had told her she would be a beneficiary."

"So who *are* the beneficiaries?" Danny fell silent for a minute.

"I hope you don't mind me asking, but they could be in danger."

"You could be right. There are only two main beneficiaries now."

"I think I know who they are."

★★★★★

Pat Loosemore sat on the sofa in the villa feeling tired and bewildered. She was now the matriarch of a damaged, diminishing family and had spent the morning trying to deal with the complicated arrangements for the repatriation of her sister's body. She had hoped that Horace would help, but he seemed incapable of completing even the most simple task and was currently slumped on the opposite sofa reading the *Mallorcan Daily Bulletin*. She blamed herself for spoiling him after her husband died in a car accident when Horace was very young. Perhaps if he had had a father figure, things would have been different. As it was, he had never really amounted to anything and she felt a pang of shame and guilt. She didn't normally feel sorry for herself but now she sat in silence wondering how life had gone so terribly wrong for the family she'd been born into.

A telephone call from Clare stirred Horace. She told him that something awful was happening in Deià, and that she was on her way there.

"Can you take Mum to our hotel?" Horace held his hand over the phone, relaying Clare's request to his mother. She nodded, but looked unhappy at the suggestion. Horace rang off and decided he should try to cheer her up.

"Come on, Mum. Things aren't all bad. You'll enjoy Deià, the final resting place of Robert Graves. Picasso once lived there as well."

"Yes dear, that does sound nice." She didn't sound convinced.

Horace persisted, "I'll take you for lunch at La Residencia tomorrow, they've got a lovely restaurant on the terrace looking down at the valley and out to sea. We could share one of their paellas, full of prawns and mussels, and we'll wash it down with a nice bottle of Rioja. What could be better?"

Pat tried to smile knowing Horace meant well but she also knew he would probably drink the whole bottle himself.

"It's very odd, you know, a very odd business!" Pat announced as they set off.

"What in particular?" Horace took the scenic, mountain route, hoping his mother would enjoy the spectacular views.

"Alison, her behaviour in all this. And now she's disappeared. When we were growing up she was always such a dear, sweet little girl."

"Danny thinks she's been kidnapped."

"I wonder if she's stage-managed it." Horace was surprised by his mother's suggestion but her attention was then caught by a stray goat hobbling along the roadside towards them, and nothing more was said about it.

★★★★★

The officers at the *Policià Local de Puerto Portals* were making progress. The grey Citröen they were tracking had been discovered, abandoned in a quiet residential street in Santa Ponça. There was no sign of the gang and no sign of Alison Galvin. There had yet to be a ransom demand, but they expected one at any moment. Danny, on his way to another meeting with Martin Whitlock, was not impressed.

"Have you no other leads? I mean, how many gangs have you got going around kidnapping old ladies?"

"Enough," came the curt reply.

"Well keep me informed." He finished the call and decided there and then to contact Osvaldo and Diego.

Martin Whitlock ushered Danny straight into his office with a gathering motion of his hand.

"Conclusive, it's conclusive. The will's legal. Your father's doctor has just confirmed to me he was in sound mind; the money, the inheritance, is yours and Sharon's to share. We'll prepare the necessary paperwork."

"Thanks, that's very good news. Sharon's on her way here, arriving tomorrow I think. Have you heard from anyone else about the will?"

"Yes, I had a call from Monika a few days ago."

"What did she want?"

"Her legacy. She claimed it had all been sorted out ages ago. She said Peter, er, Paul told her and Don Davenport."

"How did she react to your telling her?"

"She became very angry and said I'd be hearing from Mr Davenport, but now he and your father are dead, she's rather short of options." His voice trailed off.

"So she's kidnapped my mother!"

"What?" Whitlock blinked, staring at Danny in disbelief. Every time he spoke to him he heard another extraordinary development. "So we'll probably receive a ransom demand. Monika knows we are handling Paul Galvin's estate. It'll probably come here." Danny nodded but thought he detected a sad tone in Whitlock's voice, as if this would be a defeat for him personally. "Is there anything else I should know, so I'm as forewarned as possible?"

"How do you mean?" Danny decided to withhold the news of Diana's suicide.

"Well, for instance, do you know what's happened to your cousin since he escaped police custody? D'you have any idea where he is?"

"Not right now. He broke into a shop in Deià where his girlfriend, Leia works, tied her up and stole some money and then got away ."

"Where's his girlfriend now?"

"She's recovering. Clare's with her."

"Has anyone asked Leia where Roope might have gone?"
"Well, they tried … "

"And?"

"She's so traumatised that at the moment she can't speak. She's become mute!"

Martin Whitlock rolled his head back in his seat, nothing this client told him surprised him anymore. Danny got up wearily, stuck out his hand to bid him goodbye and walked out of the office to his car. He turned to see Whitlock standing at the window watching him leave.

CHAPTER ELEVEN

Blindfolded, Alison Galvin walked hesitantly with her arms outstretched in front of her. She had no idea where she was. Monika assured her that everything would be all right and to just take two more steps.

"Where am I? Who are you people?" She tried to make her voice sound steadier than she felt.

"We'll look after you but you need to stay calm."

"Stay calm! I can't see!"

Monika became distressed by her state, thinking there was no need for Mrs Galvin to be detained like this. Looking around anxiously, she decided to remove the blindfold. Blinking at the bright light, Alison saw she was in a bedroom, but she had no idea where.

"Alison, it's me, Monika, you know, Peter's friend."

A scruffy, unshaven man in his mid-twenties sauntered into the room and yawned lazily, not bothering to cover his mouth.

"Why's her blindfold off?" Monika flinched, explaining, "Andrzej, this old lady isn't going to run away. She's got no idea where she is!"

"But she bait, she must do as we say!" Andrzej shrugged, knowing Monika was probably right.

"Yes, she's bait, but she'll do as we say, she's way too old to run away. We need to keep her well, make phone call." The door bell rang. Simultaneously, Andrzej heard his mobile ring.

"Yes?" he shouted at the locked door.

"Can I come in?" The voice sounded desperate.

"Who the fuck are you?"

"A friend of Leia's."

"Leia." Andrzej slowly pronounced her name. He inched open the door. A man's outstretched hand, clutching a stash of Euros, greeted him. Andrzej ignored it.

"So why you here? Why Leia send you?" He opened the door further and ushered the visitor inside, watching him very carefully. Alison strained to overhear the conversation coming from the hallway. She caught snatches – "Can get you to mainland but you pay, first then we see!" She heard an English voice reply, "I can pay but I must know where I land, who I meet," and felt that it was vaguely familiar.

"You pay me mister, properly, and I let you go with Illie, but you fuck with me you don't go …"

"How much?"

"Two thousand Euros." Then the penny dropped and Alison recognized the voice. It belonged to Guy Roope. At that moment Monika was looking down at her phone so Alison seized her chance. She stood up and limped as quickly as she could to the door.

"Guy?" Roope stepped back, appalled. Alison noticed the bandage around his wrist, and the wild look in his eyes.

"Guy, is it really, really you?" Monika, leapt to her feet and grabbed Alison's arm.

"Mrs Galvin, you must come back in here. You're in danger."

"Aunt Alison," Guy recovered, swiftly switching on his charm, "how nice to see you again!"

"You know old lady?" Andrzej said angrily. He was furious their location could now be compromised by this unscheduled arrival.

"Yes, indeed. She's my favourite Aunty. And tell me, how is Don?" He could still feel Davenport's neck between his hands.

"Oh Guy. He's dead!" Alison wailed.

"Oh my God!" Roope leapt forward to console her. Even Monika felt moved to tears. Andrzej sprang forward:

"Okay, none of this my problem," he turned to Guy, "You do as I say." He glared at him "Who the fuck are you? What's your name?"

"Guy Roope." He made sure he kept a compassionate smile fixed on his distraught aunt. He was wondering how he was going to get the two thousand Euros it would cost him to get to the mainland, given his snatch from the shop was only a paltry two hundred and eighty Euros. He needed to get his aunt to help him. Andrzej turned back to Roope.

"So, who are you? What did you say to Monika?" He paused but before Roope could reply he continued, "And you say Leia sent you, now this lady your favourite Auntie? You think I born yesterday. What game you play?" Andrzej gave a loud whistle summoning two tough-looking characters into the room. Guy didn't need telling they weren't going to be his friends.

*****

"Any news on Roope?" Justyn patrolled the bedroom floor. "He could be anywhere. You know he might come after Leia again. How is she?" He turned to Clare.

"Not great, JS. The doctor's prescribed tranquilisers. He thinks she'll recover her voice once the trauma subsides. The police think she's trying to protect him."

"Did they think to ask her to write it all down?"

"Don't think so."

"Think we should?" Clare frowned, realising they should have. When Leia suddenly appeared at their bedroom door, Clare rushed over to give her a hug. Early morning tea arrived and she led Leia by the hand to a seat by a small table. Leia smiled, resting her arms on the table, keeping her head still. They watched as she stroked her face as if checking all essential features were still in place. Justyn tapped a biro gently on the table.

"Leia, we know you've had a terrible shock." Pausing, he placed his hand on Leila's arm, hoping for her attention. "But please write on this sheet of paper where you think Guy might be. I mean, apart from anything else, I would like my Harley back!" Justyn smiled self-consciously, trying to ease the tension. Leia looked up at both of them in turn, then started nodding her head like a puppet, They could see she was trying to speak. Justyn was distracted by a call from Danny.

"Yeah Dan?"

"Hi, just to let you know, I'm losing confidence in the police. I'm hiring the Argentinians again." Justyn peered over the top of his glasses at Clare. She was stroking Leia's arm, soothing her.

"Yeah, well, can't say I blame you." He moved into the corridor. "Any leads?"

"Well Osvaldo has a pretty good idea. He tells me there's a Romanian gang who come over from the mainland, rifle through villas and apartments, then go back later in the day, chucking away what they don't want as they go."

"That sounds like snatch raids. I don't think your Mum's been a victim of that. I think we're dealing with something much more professional. Also we're trying to find out from Leia where Roope might have gone. We think he might be trying to hook up with some sort of gang. Leia nodded when I suggested it. They must have a safe house somewhere, some sort of HQ, you know, a proper base."

"Yeah, Osvaldo thinks they possibly have two; a flat in a rundown area not far from the airport and a house in the middle of nowhere."

"Shouldn't we work with the police now?"

"Possibly, look ..." Clare appeared in the corridor, clutching a piece of paper in her left hand, jabbing at it with her right index finger.

"Hang on." He held his hand over the mouthpiece. "Yes?"

"Look, Leia's written down 'ANDRZEJ'; she's gone back to her room. I think she's looking for something else, perhaps we'll have better details soon."

Justyn finished his call.

"I'll ring you when we know more, Dan." To their dismay Leia re-appeared, crying.

"Don't tell me, Guy took your address book?" Leia nodded, she'd been so traumatised in the shop, she hadn't noticed him sweeping it up as he left.

"Don't worry, darling." Clare embraced her. Leia's phone rang. She pressed answer.

"Hi, babes, it's Andrzej, you Okay?" Leia grimaced, stabbing her finger at the name she'd written on the piece of paper Clare was holding; she quickly passed the phone to Clare who squeaked, "Yes?"

"Good, didn't think you wanted me back in your life, babes. But you sent big Englishman, yes?"

"So, where are you Andrzej?" Clare attempted another impersonation of Leia.

"Wait minute, this not my Leia!" Clare lost her nerve and shoved the phone back at Leia, who quickly pressed 'end call.' She looked terrified. Justyn and Clare exchanged urgent glances,

"Leia, can we borrow your mobile for ten minutes?"

Leia looked defeated and handed it to Justyn, "Thanks. I'll do it. You stay with Leia." Clare nodded. Justyn rushed across the corridor and hobbled down two flights of stairs as fast as his painful hip would allow. Once out of the hotel he turned left and headed towards the police station.

He was so out of breath when he got there that he could hardly get the words out to the duty officer to explain what had happened. In desperation he pointed to the mobile and stuttered, "Last call, gangster, kidnap …" To his enormous surprise and relief the officer lifted his hand, stopping him in his tracks, and gestured to him to hand over the phone. He then took it into one of the back offices and asked Justyn to wait.

After a very short time another officer explained to Justyn that the call had been traced to a caller in Porreras and that they would be sending police cars to investigate. Justyn phoned Clare and told her what had happened and asked her to be ready in her car, as he was on his way back.

He limped back to the hotel as quickly as he could, and spotted Clare's blue Golf already parked outside. Clare was sitting in the passenger seat, with Leia looking nervous in the back. He climbed into the driver's side and sped off in pursuit of the two police cars, which had, helpfully set their sirens blaring.

★★★★★

Pat picked at some loose skin on her forefinger, deep in thought, determined more than ever to find her younger sister, Alison, whose betrayal she now considered had indirectly led to the suicide of her other sister, Diana. Neither she, nor Horace, had any idea where Clare was heading as they followed her out of Deià. Clare noticed them within the first few minutes, the twisting corners on the road out towards Valldemossa gave plenty of opportunity to see who was behind. She decided not to share her observation with Justyn and Leia. They already had enough to worry about.

Back at the hideaway, Andrzej exploded with rage, "Illie!" he yelled at his colleague, "The bitch, the bitch Leia, she tells Englishman to come here and now I think she tells *policía*."

"How do you know, boss?" Illie asked.

"I call her, she gives phone to other bitch who pretends to be her … she probably with police …"

"What we do?"

"Get out now!" With that he flung open the back door and threw his mobile as far as he could onto some broken concrete. "We move fast, Monika!" he shouted "tie old lady, put blindfold, Illie shoot Englishman!"

"I don't think so!" Andrzej spun round, to find Roope holding a knife at Monika's throat. Andrzej was startled. He couldn't understand how Roope had got away from Illie nor how he had got hold of a knife. He could see that Roope was serious. He had the look of a killer.

"You don't want to hurt nice lady, she sweet, she can be sweet to you." Monika, knew what he meant.

"Shut up! Get that baboon to get me on his boat now or she gets it!"

There was a crash of splintered glass behind them.

"Luka …. you check …" Andrzej and Roope kept their eyes fixed on each other.

"Boss, old lady has smashed window. Think throw something at it. She angry but still here."

Luka's attention was suddenly taken by a noise outside. Luka turned off the lights and saw a car parked some twenty yards away on the scrubland beyond the house.

"Who is it, Luka?" Andrzej asked, anxiously.

"Don't know, boss," Luka whispered, "but they drive Mercedes Sports."

"They certainly do," Guy announced, guessing it was the Argentinian pair, Osvaldo and Diego; it occurred to him that they could be his salvation. His luck was in. "So, you see my Argentine friends are here, they won't like it if you don't play ball."

Andrzej was sweating. He feared these Argentinians more than any other gang, and certainly more than the police. Briefly, he thought of cutting a deal with Roope, but couldn't let it involve Monika. He needed Monika to help get the ransom for releasing Alison Galvin.

"Guy!" It was Alison's desperate cry for help from the other room. Guy heard it just as all the lights went out.

★★★★★

Justyn switched off the car's lights. Dusk was falling as he slowed to a stop on waste ground immediately behind the police car he'd followed from Deià. In his rear view mirror he saw Horace pull up behind him, his mother looking gaunt and anxious in the passenger seat. He watched another car pull up, seeing Danny at the wheel. He turned the engine off. He resisted looking at Clare. He could hear her breathing, he knew she was nervous. Leia, sitting directly behind her, buried her head in her hands.

"It's all my fault – I should never have given Guy this address."

"Ssh, it's alright." But as Justyn spoke he became aware of five vehicles slowly passing him with their lights turned off. He was sure they were all police vehicles, although some were unmarked. He watched them pass some derelict buildings and heard them crunch on gravel as they approached a house. They stopped abruptly. Justyn glanced at Clare. They knew the police had found the house.

"Who's that, over there?" Clare paused. All three watched as two shapes moved gingerly away from the house.

"Oh my God, it's Alison. She's being helped by someone."

"Monika!" Leia whispered.

Danny appeared at Justyn's window.

"Jump in." The four remained silent, until Danny spotted his mother.

"Stay put," Justyn barked, "it's far too dangerous."

"It's the Argentinians!" Clare blurted out, recognising two characters running around the side of the house.

The police needed no further invitation. They leapt out of their cars and ran towards the building; one with a loud hailer shouting: "Quedense donde estan. Que no se mueva nadie!"

In the mayhem, Danny thrust his door open and rushed out of the car towards his mother. "Quedénse atrás!" came the order through the loud hailer and he could only watch helplessly as his mother and Monika were escorted away.

The police stormed their way into the house. Justyn froze when he saw the two Argentinians running towards his car. He locked the door but they ran past at full pelt away from the house. The police were too distracted to see them as they broke into a sprint.

After the initial bedlam, the house fell silent. Justyn, out of the corner of his eye, noticed Danny disappearing from view. Startled by a hand tapping on his window; he wound it down.

"Leia, it is Leia isn't it?" A *policía* peered into the back of the car. He demanded that Leia get out. "We need you, please." Leia climbed out, trembling.

"We'll come too," Clare jumped out, threading her arm through Leia's. Justyn was quickly by her side.

"You're safe now," the *policía* reassured Leia, "safe now," he repeated. Removing Clare's arm, he gently but firmly led Leia into the house. Clare and Justyn followed immediately behind.

As they entered they were confronted by a man lying face down in a pool of blood. The *policía* rolled him onto his side. Leia staggered forward and screamed, seeing the knife embedded in the man's throat.

Justyn eased her carefully onto a sofa.

"It's Andrzej." Leia whispered.

The *policía* nodded, "Does he work alone?"

Leia opened her mouth, but no words came out. She leant forward and could just be heard saying, "No, never, he always has Illie and Luka with him."

By now the police had completed their search and turned their attention to the surrounding areas, their torches on full beam.

Justyn and Clare turned again to Leia. "Where's Guy?" they heard her whisper.

One of the policeman led Leia, Monika and Alison Galvin to a marked car that was waiting to drive them to the station at Palma for questioning. As they were escorted away, they heard orders being shouted for the docks to be searched.

Danny looked nervously at his mother. Whatever the sins of the past, what he saw now was a frail and frightened old woman. He wanted to hug her.

"I'll come with you." He rushed to join her.

The ambulance drew up outside with its lights still flashing. Andrzej was stretchered out with a blanket covering him from top to toe. Justyn feared repercussions would follow. Andrzej, according to Leia, was the leader of a very dangerous gang. He suspected his death would not go unpunished.

"Clare and I will follow you. Is that Okay Dan?" They exchanged nervous looks, both keen to leave the scene as quickly as possible.

On arriving at the police station, Justyn took stock: Alison, looking like a ghost was waiting outside an interview room while Monika who was babbling non-stop was led away to be questioned. Leia sat next to him, whispering "He's out there, he's still out there." An officer overheard her.

"It's alright, lady, you're with us now. No one can harm you."

The door swung wide open and Horace strode confidently into the room with his mother behind him. Joining Leia, Justyn and Clare, Pat arrived in time to see Alison being led away, but before she disappeared into a room Pat marched straight over to her. The policeman who was with Alison felt powerless to stop this formidable woman from having her say.

"What happened to you? What happened to that nice little girl? Do you remember when we chased each other around the daffodils at home in Saxmundham? What on earth happened to you?" Alison met her gaze, but couldn't find words. As Pat watched Alison being led away she yelled, "You and me and Diana pretending we were playing 'Swallows and Amazons'? Remember? Where did you go, why did you betray us?" Alison missed Pat's last question as the interview room door clanged shut behind her. "Come on Ali, you must have something to say?" Pat shouted at the closed door.

Danny shifted uncomfortably in his seat and turned to his cousin Horace, hoping he could calm his mother down. But Justyn took over.

"I'm sure, Pat, you have every right to ask these questions but there's a lot going on and we're more worried about what might happen next." Pat looked blank.

"You see, Diana's boy, Guy," Justyn continued, "is still on the run. We think he's killed someone else."

Pat began to take in what Justyn was saying and sank into a stunned silence.

"He put knife in throat!" Monika bellowed as she was led back to them, now released from custody. They all turned, aghast, to look at her.

"What?"

Monika didn't see who said it.

"Roope put knife in Andrzej throat! He had knife at my neck.

Then lights go out when Andrzej shouts. Roope puts knife where he hears voice."

Pat swallowed hard and struggled to her feet.

"I think I might ..." Unable to steady herself, she lurched forward for a few steps, and then folded rather elegantly to the floor. Clare quickly gathered her up and walked slowly with her to find some water and a more comfortable place to wait.

"What about my Argentinian friends, Monika what did *they* do?" asked Danny.

"They rescued me and your mother, Danny. I think they fused lights. They good people." Danny sighed, relieved they had actually helped. After all that had happened, he felt a little skip of joy that he, alone, had contributed something positive. Monika excused herself and went to see what had happened to Clare and Pat.

Some ten minutes later Alison was escorted back to them and Pat returned, and surprised even herself, by stretching out her hand. Alison gratefully took it. Pat stepped closer, holding her sister's gaze, then pulled her to her in a warm embrace.

"Thank you, thank you Pat, I've been so wicked, so wicked. I wouldn't blame you if you never wanted to see me again, if you'd wanted to kill me." Pat smiled weakly, not really knowing what she thought anymore.

"Well, we need to know what happens now." The elderly sisters both turned to look at Justyn who again felt the need to take the initiative. Justyn looked at Danny.

"Yes, I know a man who can help. Martin Whitlock. He's a solicitor in Valldemossa." Danny had taken the cue.

"I know him." Alison interrupted. "I want to see him as soon as possible, to arrange for Grandpa's money to be properly split." No one could believe what they were hearing. Pat got up and hugged her. Alison buried her face in her sister's shoulder and burst into loud, uncontrollable sobs. Danny left the room to ring Whitlock. He skipped the preliminaries and got straight to the point.

"I need to see you again, but this time I'll bring Mum and Aunt Pat with me."

Clare appeared and was waving at him that she had something to say. "Hold on a minute."

"Sharon has landed in Palma. I thought you'd want to know. She's been trying to get hold of you."

"Thanks." Danny then resumed his call with Whitlock. "Sorry about that. In fact my sister Sharon has just arrived so she will be coming to our meeting as well. That makes six of us."

"But tell me about the kidnapping. What's been going on? What happened to them? Where's Monika?" There was no disguising the concern in Whitlock's voice.

"One dead, the main man, two on the run!"

"Your cousin, Guy Roope?"

"Not dead and on the run."

Whitlock hesitated before enquiring: "And Monika, is she one of the two on the run?"

"No, she's with us here at Palma Police Station. She turned tables on the others and helped Mum escape. She and Mum have been released and are sitting with us now."

"Good." For the first time Danny detected something not quite right. He couldn't quite put his finger on it. He confirmed the time for the morning meeting and rang off.

★★★★★

As soon as Leia's head hit the pillow, she fell into a deep sleep. She was exhausted by everything that had happened and by turning things over and over in her mind in a desperate attempt to make sense of her fascination with Guy. Would he have killed her? Was he a monster? Why didn't she want to believe it? It was reassuring that Justyn and Clare's bedroom was immediately across the corridor and they had told her to call them if anything disturbed or worried her.

Danny knew it was going to be extremely difficult to reconcile his mother with his sister but he started by putting them in a twin room. He lied that it was the only one available. Initially Sharon had been aloof and struggled to switch into Happy Families mode after twenty years in the wilderness. She resented beyond words their father's betrayal. Danny tried to amuse and relax them and soon peals of laughter were heard down the corridor. Danny felt it would now be safe to leave them together and that the two bottles of Vina Sol had been an extremely good investment. He returned to his room and phoned Osvaldo.

"Hey, hombre, you did well!" He hoped that was the cool way to talk to these guys, although he had no idea. They probably thought he was some stupid wet-behind-the-ears Englishman who didn't know what the hell he was doing and they would probably be right.

"Where Roope? He disappeared?"

"So did you, according to the police … but hey, you did nothing wrong. You helped them. They want to see you guys, tomorrow at Palma HQ."

"Cojones! We meet you, ginger man, but no police. Text where." The line went dead. Danny was sufficiently savvy to know that Osvaldo and Diego would never help the police with any enquiries but he felt if he were ever asked, at least he had tried. He texted Osvaldo with the rendezvous point where he would pay them and added: *don't worry, no police will be there!*

A few hours later Leia awoke, sure she'd heard noises in the corridor outside her room. Lying still, almost stiff with fear, she strained her ears, but could only hear the sound of the aging air-conditioning unit humming in the background. She began to regret turning down an offer of a police guard. She assumed that because Justyn and Clare had been there for her so much, they would continue to protect her now. Justyn had quite literally saved her life at the shop and she felt so close to Clare, who had become a sort of mother figure. That feeling made Leia think of Angie, her real mother. She'd always regarded her as a sort of angel – otherworldly, unburdened by material possessions, a free spirit who lived and loved without boundaries. When Leia was small she would play and sing Leonard Cohen's 'Suzanne' and she remembered hearing about 'tea and oranges that came all the way from China'. It summed up Angie. Sometimes she felt resentful. Had her mother's freewheeling, chain-smoking life contributed to her early death? And then there was her father who remained a mystery. She had never met him and had no idea who he was. Sometimes her resentment would give way to self-pity. She had never had the chance to have a good education and go to University, make something of herself. But she resisted the temptation to become bitter. She was still young; anything was still possible if she believed it was.

Her reverie was disturbed by more noises from outside. This time it was the shuffle of footsteps in the corridor. She glanced at her watch – 4.10 a.m. – and quickly texted Justyn.

Are you awake?

Yes.

Can you hear footsteps in the corridor?

Yes. Might be the night porter, checking the floors. Don't worry, next time I'll have a look.

She wondered if she should put the chain across the door but Clare had advised against it, saying she and Justyn wouldn't be able to get in if there was an emergency. Hearing a movement at the door,

Leia screamed and sat bolt upright. She heard the sound of a key opening the door. A shadowy figure entered the darkened room. Justyn heard her door open and within seconds he was banging on it, shouting: "Let me in, I know you're in there!" He shot back into his room. "Clare, wake up! Where's the spare key to Leia's room?"

Clare woke up, got out of bed and opened a drawer almost in one movement. She took out the key and handed it to Justyn. He rushed back to Leia's door and turned it in the lock. It didn't open. It had been double locked from the inside and the key was wedged in it.

"Open up, open up, or I'll call the police!" Justyn shouted, banging his fist as hard as possible, against the locked door. Doors began to open along the corridor. Danny rushed from his room, Sharon's head poked round from inside hers, alarm written on all their faces.

"I'll call the police!" said Danny.

"No, don't," the voice paused "don't, please, please don't call the police," the voice was soft, it was Leia's. It sounded calm.

"It's all Okay, we're going to open the door now, aren't we?" The voice was soothing but gently cajoling. Justyn and Danny stood shoulder to shoulder. The door clicked open and they rushed the room, astonished to find Monika sitting forlornly on the bed, wearing the look of a weary warrior facing defeat.

"I can explain, I'm so sorry to alarm you. Leia's not worried. She knows why I'm here. I can explain everything."

Leia leant across, taking Monika's hand, before kissing her on the cheek.

"Yes she can."

★★★★★

Monika looked haunted, exhausted; they all stared at her, waiting for her to speak. Sharon made her apologies and announced she was going back to bed. She didn't view this woman as any kind of threat. Clare and Danny perched on the bed next to Leia who was hugging her knees to her chest.

Again it was Justyn who took control.

"So, Monika, you'd better tell us what's going on."

"It's Guy. He said he wanted to make his life with Leia, that he would come back for her and they would have a new identity in a new place."

Leia pulled a face but no one in the room could have guessed that things weren't that simple. "He nearly killed me," she said. "If Justyn hadn't broken in I wouldn't be here now – I was in shock for about twelve hours – couldn't even speak. Why on earth would I ever agree to spend my life with that monster?" Clare leant across to Leia, and gave her a hug.

Monika explained that Guy had told her he had to tie and bind Leia so tightly in order to buy a bit of time, but he knew Justyn was outside, and would untie her quickly. He was insistent he would never hurt Leia. Leia actually believed this to be true, but she also knew Guy was more than capable of hurting others. She tried hard to hide her anguish by hunching her knees even tighter to her chest.

"Okay Monika, if this is true and we don't presume to say you are making it up, why disturb Leia in the middle of the night?" Justyn looked down, checking his watch, it was 4.25 a.m. "I mean, couldn't it have waited until morning?"

"Guy's on the run now and may even be in Deià."

"We know he's on the run, but I doubt he's in Deià," Danny interrupted, "Mum told me he was angling to get to the docks or a port. She seemed a bit confused as to how but said he was planning it with the Eastern Europeans."

"Illie and Luka!" Monika shook her head, laughing mockingly. "Don't think they would have helped him in any way. They would

likely shoot him. Both had guns, would never have helped him!"
Justyn nodded in agreement. He thanked Monika and stood up to
go, gently motioning with his hand at Clare that she should follow
him. "Just one other thing." Monika's weak and uncertain voice now
sounded more assertive.

"Yes?" They replied in unison.

"One other reason I needed to do this, you know, tonight." All
eyes were fixed on her. "I'm pregnant." Clare and Leia gasped. Justyn
and Danny exchanged bored glances. This news could definitely
have waited until the morning.

"Is it Dad's?" Danny frowned as he spoke, fearing the answer
could once again torpedo his family back into more turmoil.

"No."

"Is it Guy's?" Clare asked.

Then in a almost inaudible whisper Monika said, "It's Martin's.
Martin Whitlock's."

"Whitlock's!" Danny sounded relieved. At least there would be
no addition to the Galvin family.

"Congratulations!" Clare's compassion got the better of her.

"When? I mean, when's the baby due?" Danny asked the
question. He remembered his last conversation with Whitlock, who
surprised him by asking after Monika. The penny was beginning to
drop. "How long, Monika? How long has your relationship with
Whitlock been going on?" Again Monika lowered her head. The
question seemed to drain strength again from her.

"Long enough." she uttered. Clare, seeing her frailty, suggested
she would try to get her a room.

"Let her sleep here." Leia intervened. "This bed can easily take
two of us. Anyway, we should stop interrogating Monika now."
For the first time Monika smiled as she felt she was with friends.
Clare pecked her on the cheek and Justyn and Danny bid quiet but

respectful 'goodnights'.

Monika lifted herself off the bed and wedged a thin cushion under the door to stop it shutting, telling Leia she would be back in a minute. Descending two flights of stairs, she returned the master key to the rack above Gregor's, the night porter's, head. He didn't stir. She suspected he was pretending to be asleep as she knew all too well that Gregor had once been part of Andrzej's gang. For a small fee, he had happily given Monika access to the master key. Knowing better than to cross anyone associated with Andrzej's circle, he kept his head bowed.

Back in their room, Justyn and Clare couldn't sleep.

"I suppose Monika heard at the police station that Danny, Sharon and Alison were all going to see Whitlock with Pat and Horace."

"Yes and that was quite something, Alison announcing she was going to put everything right. About time too, and all thanks to you JS." Clare leaned across and kissed him warmly on the lips.

"I guess Monika thought it was time things were put right for her too." Clare murmured as she drifted into sleep.

In her room across the corridor, Leia couldn't help watching Monika undress. Her underwear was skimpy to say the least, but even more eye catching was a huge tattoo of a cockerel above her left buttock. Before she climbed into bed, Monika quickly sent a text: *They know.* Monika turned to Leia, feeling she owed her friend an explanation.

"I went to Puerto Portals to tell Andrzej I no longer wanted any involvement with his gang. Told him I'm pregnant, going to start a family with the man I love, going to make new life. He was horrible, he laughed, then he shouted, 'You are never free of me and don't ever forget you owe me'. He told me he would find me wherever I went, that I would never be safe. Then he saw Mrs Galvin and told me to wait. He had been trailing her for some time. He said if I helped him kidnap Mrs Galvin, he would set me free. I went along with it, but I soon saw how cruel it was." She looked across at Leia, but she was already fast asleep. Under her breath she muttered, "We're not safe here."

CHAPTER TWELVE

The new day in Valldemossa was dreamily hazy, the veiled sunlight announcing an autumnal morning. Sitting silently, Martin Whitlock heard the clock in the square strike nine. In an hour's time he would be welcoming to his office the most bizarre group of people he had ever had to work with. In his many years as a solicitor he had dealt with countless cases of disputed wills and family feuds, but this was the most complex yet and he was still far from sure how it was going to end. He was expecting Danny Galvin, a client he liked and had got to know quite well, Danny's sister Sharon and their mother Alison. Then there would be the Loosemores, Pat and her son and daughter, Horace and Clare and finally he had invited a potential beneficiary, his lover, Monika. He'd prepared for her to attend and she told him she would be there but his text asking for confirmation had not been answered. Would she actually dare to turn up and fight her corner? As ten o'clock approached, Martin heard a text arrive on his phone. It was from Monika.

Am in police custody in Palma, arrested at 5 a.m.

A cold sensation ran through him.

He quickly texted back: *Are you Okay? What's happened?*

Yes, Okay, but police find two dead bodies in the water – Luka and Illie – Andrzej's gang – so bring me in as I was at kidnap house.

Stay strong.

Okay

★★★★★

Monika's arrest had deeply affected Leia. She waited until first light, at around 7.30 a.m., and contacted Osvaldo. Clare had explained to her how Danny had hired them to track down his mother, Alison and her companion, Don Davenport. She admitted she had tried to hire them as well but Danny had beaten her to it. Now Leia needed them. She couldn't tell Justyn. He was protecting her, watching her. But she needed to find Monika. Perched on a table in the corner of Justyn's room, she watched the movement of vehicles in and out of the hotel car park. Before long she spotted the Mercedes Sports slowing down, turning left off the road and into the car park. She watched them alight, Osvaldo and the one Clare called 'Scarface'. Justyn was in the bathroom so she called out she was going back to her room to get something.

"Okay, but don't shut any doors."

He thought it highly unlikely Guy was lurking around at this time, but he felt an acute responsibility for Leia, knowing how traumatised she had been. He also knew Clare trusted him to keep her safe. He emerged from the bathroom and called her name. There was no reply so he ran across to her room shouting "Leia!"

The room was empty and, as he got to the window, he just caught sight of the Mercedes Sports accelerating out of the car park and turning right onto the road to Valdemossa. He thought he could see Leia in the back seat. And then he realised there was absolutely nothing he could do. Clare had taken her Golf to the meeting with Whitlock and the Harley-Davidson was still missing. He phoned Clare, but she had switched her mobile off. Danny was in the same meeting and uncontactable. Even Horace, who could have made himself useful for once, was locked in the same meeting. He dialled Reception and asked them to call a taxi to take him to Palma Police Station. He had no evidence Leia would have gone there, but it was a hunch. He had to hope that Leia had hired the Argentinians. It appeared she'd got into their car of her own free will. Would they double cross her, might they deliver her to Roope?

*****

Whitlock poured boiling water onto the teabag in his cup, as he contemplated the meeting. He knew the UK Law Society would deem him 'unprofessional' for having a relationship with a client. But was she a client? Yes, by association, she was. He was looking forward to parenthood with Monika, despite all the complications. Deep down he knew he was bored of his way of life and had at last done something about it.

He thought back to the first time he had seen Monika. It was at lunch at Paul Galvin's luxurious villa overlooking the valley in Deià. She had fussed around as they sat discussing Paul's affairs on the outside terrace. Her role had appeared to fall between two stools; she left the preparation and delivery of the lunch to others, but wasn't invited to join them at the table. Half way through their meal, he glanced down to see her swimming in the pool and when she climbed out of the water he was struck by how attractive she was. He was sure Monika was looking up, checking if he was watching and he began to wonder if that had been the point of the swim. The situation was complicated by the fact that Paul, her employer and companion, had just told him he didn't think he had long to live.

"She's a special girl," Paul told him, while both men watched her reclining on a sun lounger. "She'll need looking after. I'd like to bequeath a legacy for her."

He'd asked Whitlock to set up an annuity of a hundred thousand Euros for the next ten years. As their plates were cleared, Paul announced he needed his afternoon siesta. He rose to his feet carefully, picked up his inhaler, and hobbled back towards the villa with Whitlock following behind. At the drawing room entrance Paul turned back.

"Why don't you make her acquaintance? Tell her about the process. She knows what I'm planning."

Whitlock felt uncomfortable. He knew Paul's estate was controlled by a trust and he envisaged problems with the co-trustee, Don Davenport, who had never given him a permanent address, but was always making it clear he controlled Paul Galvin. Deciding there was no time like the present, Whitlock went down to the pool to talk to Monika. He felt rather self-conscious sitting on a sun lounger fully clothed next to a beautiful woman in a bikini. He began to broach the subject of the possible legacy and the problem with Davenport but was taken aback when Monika brushed the problems aside and said she would speak to Davenport herself. Whitlock meekly concurred. Standing up to go, she smiled and kissed him on both cheeks. As she walked away, Whitlock couldn't help noticing a large tattoo of a cockerel above her left buttock.

He had been living alone in Mallorca since his wife had abandoned him ten years earlier. He had been crushed when she walked out accusing him of being a stuffed shirt and having ruined her life. He had never really recovered. After leaving him she got involved with a much more glamorous ex-pat set in Puerto Portals, dominated by Howard Marks, the charismatic Welsh drug smuggler. Martin did not approve but would sometimes drive there, often spotting her amongst a prosperous looking group of diners at 'Wellies', their favourite restaurant by the quay. On one fateful occasion he had dared to approach her at an upstairs table. She was surrounded by her new friends and on seeing him, she had dismissed him with a cursory wave of her hand. He never went there again.

As he drove back to Valldemossa after his meeting at Paul Galvin's villa, he knew Monika had stirred something. After his long period of enforced celibacy, he desired her in a way he had assumed he would never experience again. He knew it was wrong. It would break every code he lived by, but it was distracting and intoxicating.

A clandestine meeting with Monika at his house near Banyalbufar soon followed. It had been easy enough to arrange as she always answered Paul's phone. His coded messages started with a date, time and place where he would collect her and if she could make the rendezvous she would make a 'click' noise before handing the phone to Paul.

Some weeks later, whilst making his new will, Paul told Martin about his son Danny and that he was on the island. With tears in his eyes he admitted the whole story of his faked death and the terrible guilt he felt at the deception he'd perpetrated. Martin was shocked by what he heard and wrestled with his conscience as to what to do with all this information, but decided it was not for him to judge his clients. He liked Paul, and he persuaded himself that in the interest of client confidentiality he could legitimately keep the information to himself. When Paul then revealed he was terminally ill, the problem seemed to be solving itself. Whitlock was pleased to help him write a further will but remained wary of Davenport, knowing he had to tell him about it. He also knew that making a new will for the assets in Paul's sole name would be legally binding, if it was concluded quickly while Paul was still of sound mind. A doctor's 'mental capacity test' would soon fix that. Knowing time could be short, Whitlock hand-wrote the new will.

"So, your children are now the beneficiaries, let's add the legacy for Monika."

Galvin's eyes narrowed, giving away the second thoughts he now had. Why was his solicitor so concerned for Monika?

"No" he replied, "I've changed my mind."

The words had shocked Whitlock. He snapped out of his reverie.

The family had arrived. They ended up squashed around a table that was much too small and they made for a motley crowd. It was hard to believe they were related. Looking round the table he marvelled at the power of money. How divisive it is and how quickly it can bring warring factions together when there's some prospect of a pay-out.

"Welcome everybody and thank you all for coming today. I really hope we can get through things fairly quickly as I'm sure some of you have only just arrived and must be quite tired."

Danny piped up:

"It's not been the best of nights. Finally got settled at 4.30 a.m. then the *policias* burst in at 5 a.m. and arrested Monika!"

Whitlock realised that he must remain professional and keep focused on the task at hand. He invited Alison Galvin to speak first. She announced falteringly, at first, then more confidently, that she wanted to redistribute the money she had inherited from her father, the late Ken Stone. The group sat listening intently, gripped as Alison set about righting the sins of the past. "And the house, Stone Manor at Saxmundham – we've let it all these years – Don did it through an agent – but I've got the paperwork. I'd like to return there and share it with you, Pat."

To everyone's huge embarrassment Horace leapt to his feet to wrap his arms around his mother, while Pat merely dabbed her eyes with a tissue, just about managing to whisper, "Thank you."

Whitlock, grateful to be getting through the meeting, explained the necessary legal processes that would follow: "Deeds of Assignment, Special Legacies. It'll take a while but it's all doable now Davenport is dead." Alison sighed. He turned to her, "I'm sorry, Mrs Galvin, but with Mr Davenport's unfortunate death there are fewer complications."

He couldn't bring himself to offer condolences on her loss, and noticed what he thought were appreciative looks on the faces of the others. At that moment Clare noticed a message from Justyn on her mobile and shrieked;

"What?"

"Leia's disappeared!"

*****

Clare abruptly ended the meeting with Whitlock. Danny, ashen -faced, rushed to join her. Sharon ran to catch up but Danny held up his hand and advised her it was safer to stay away. He would ring to update as soon as he could.

Whitlock was left standing in the doorway; aghast yet again at this latest development, he meekly requested: "Please keep me posted. Hope you find Leia … and Monika."

Clare and Danny figured if Roope had taken Leia, he'd have headed to Puerto Portals. The fast boat that had been organised earlier in the week could have been re-activated. Forty minutes later they were running down the jetty, eyes anxiously screening the moored vessels. Clare phoned Justyn.

"We're at the quay at Puerto Portals, no sign of either of them."

"Who?"

"Leia or Roope."

"They were never going to be there!"

"Why are you so certain? Where are you?"

"At the police station at Palma. I suspect Leia wants to vouch for Monika."

*****

Monika looked drawn and diminished as she walked gingerly down the steps from the police station. Leia had vouched for her innocence, giving evidence of her positive action in the collapse of Alison Galvin's kidnap; but it was only after a call to Alison herself that the *policías* decided to release her. The bodies found floating in the sea had been identified as Illie and Luka, Andrzej's two cronies. Finally, the police decided it had nothing to do with Monika, revealing their search was now to find Roope as quickly as possible.

Leia had waited with Danny, Clare and Justyn. She rushed forward to greet her friend. They embraced and moved away from the group, talking earnestly to one another.

"We're going to go away." Monika announced to Clare in particular, but not caring if Danny and Justyn heard. "To my country, Poland," she continued, "I'll call for Martin when our baby's due. We think it safer to get out of Mallorca now … " Clare looked at Leia who nodded in agreement.

CHAPTER THIRTEEN

Three Months Later
Stone Manor, Saxmundham
Christmas Eve.

"They're up here!" Clare yelled, delighted to have found the Christmas tree decorations in the loft. "Lucky I've got gloves on, they're covered in spiders' webs. They're huge!"

"Nonsense, darling," teased her mother, "Your father would have said you should have grown up in Queensland!"

Clare passed the box of decorations down to her mother who was standing half way up the ladder to the loft. Alison joined them on the landing, smiling warmly. Was this really happening? A family reunion at her father's home in a beautiful part of Suffolk? She also knew she would never be free of the guilt of her past.

"So, how many for dinner?" Clare answered her own question as they made their way downstairs. "Us three, Justyn, Horace with Annabel, Danny with Oliver, Sharon, Leia and Monika. Justyn's at Saxmundham station waiting for Leia and Monika now, and oh, how on earth could I forget, our special guest tonight, Martin Whitlock. So that makes twelve. Hope this fog won't be a problem for anyone travelling. We've got Mrs Cross back in the kitchen, with Mrs Partridge, her sister, helping her; it's so good to see them again. I'll just check if they need help."

As Pat and Alison sat in the drawing room, Justyn's green Jaguar came into view, crunching up the drive towards the house. They called to Clare that he was here and she rushed out shrieking at Leia and Monika as they got out of the car. Beaming with joy, seeing the colour and fun back in Leia's young face, Clare turned to Monika;

"So good to see you both, when's the happy…" Catching her words, taking immediate stock of Monika's flat stomach. "Oh I'm so sorry…"

"Please don't be, it wasn't meant to be. Martin's very upset about it though; anyway we've had a great journey, we took the Eurostar from Lille." Leia joined in, "What a sweet little railway station we came to, we walked back across the railway line the train was going on, when we saw Justyn in the car park! Are all stations like Sax-mund-ham?" Clare giggled at Leia's pronunciation. "Is it always misty here like this?"

"Well, welcome to Suffolk! And this is fog, not mist, Leia. We've got what we call a real 'pea-souper' coming down now!"

Clare's attention was diverted by the headlights of a vehicle, slowly navigating the twisting driveway in the increasing gloom. It turned out be a local taxi with Martin Whitlock sitting in the back. As soon as the vehicle stopped, Monika grabbed the door handle, pulled the door wide open, leant inside and almost collapsed on Martin, her eyes filling with tears.

"I came over from Orford. I met up with an old friend there," he announced rather matter-of-factly but Monika wasn't listening. She was overwhelmed with emotion, reunited with her lover at last. Clare and Leia exchanged glances and moved away quickly to give them some space.

Leia's eyes widened as she passed between stone lions on plinths and entered the Manor house. Clare led her through the hall, one end dominated by a vast, gilt-framed mirror, decorated with a holly and ivy garland, speckled with red berries. At the other end she saw the largest Christmas tree she'd ever seen. Then she noticed an impressive suit of armour on the far side wall and wondered whether it was a real sword in its sheath.

"This house was designed and built by my grandfather," Clare explained. "Really a monument to his massive ego! It's all done in the neo-Gothic style, but was actually only built in the 1960s." Leia looked back blankly. Clare, realising her words were lost on her, swiftly changed tack. "Let's talk about tonight. There'll be twelve of us, Justyn will like that, he'll think it's a cricket team with a twelfth man!" Leia frowned, never having heard of cricket. "Anyway, tonight we'll be recreating how we used to spend Christmas past, I mean as children, my brother, Horace and I, and our cousins, Danny and Sharon and … oh, I'm sorry, … yes, and I'm afraid Guy as well, but don't worry," she squeezed Leia's hand tightly, "he won't be bothering us now!" Leia looked down, struggling to find words, Clare continued, "It was so good to hear the Spanish police have pronounced him dead!"

"But no one's heard have they, how or where he died?" Leia tilted her head at Clare, anxiously searching for confirmation.

"Well, let's bury him in our minds anyway, darling, he won't be here. He's dead to all of us, the police wouldn't put out a false message anyway. Now, we always had our big Christmas meal on Christmas Eve, that's tonight, which leaves Christmas Day free for presents, church, a long walk or a visit to the beach at Aldeburgh, weather permitting. Then we'll have a late lunch back here at the Manor." Leia had never come across anything like this before and just stood wide eyed.

"But let's take you to your room."

As they climbed the grand stairway, Leia stopped at the top to study a portrait. Clare explained it was the family's patron, her grandfather, the late Ken Stone. Something about it troubled Leia. It was the eyes. She thought she saw something sinister in the eyes: her mother had always impressed on her that people's characters are revealed by their eyes. She thought Stone's were too close together and they looked mean. She glanced back at it as Clare escorted her along a seemingly endless, cold corridor, finally turning right, down a few steps and into her room. It was smaller than she had expected, with only an old metal-framed bed and a standalone wooden wardrobe; on the wall was a cheap-looking plastic clock, which she thought looked out of place and she was surprised that there were no pictures. Moving to the window, she hoped for a view, but was disappointed. The pitch black night sky and thickening fog seemed about to invade her room. She shuddered.

"Come down for drinks at 7 p.m." Clare breezily announced, pecking Leia on the cheek. It was only 5 p.m. and Leia had no idea what she would to do for the next two hours. Since she had left Deià with Monika and headed to her friend's family home in Warsaw, she had never been on her own. She was sad that she couldn't share a room with Monika, not now that Martin Whitlock was here. They had been mutually self-supporting; both feared being alone, both continued to fear Guy Roope – both were desperate for hard evidence that he was actually dead. They also feared the remnants of Andrzej's Romanian gang. They had felt safe in Warsaw. Monika seemed popular and established. Leia often wondered why Monika had moved to Mallorca in the first place. Her stock answer, 'the sunshine', never totally convinced her.

Later that evening, after drinks in the hallway, the twelve guests took their places at the dining room table. Pat Loosemore stood up. "For what we are about to receive, may the Lord make us truly thankful. Amen." She continued, "Alison and I, and our sadly departed sister, Diana, used to bring our families here every Christmas at the behest of our father, Ken – it was quite a tradition."

Justyn thought he heard a noise outside and checked Danny's face to see if he'd heard it, but seeing no reaction, he returned his attention back to Pat; "It was also our tradition to have our Christmas meal, our dinner, on Christmas Eve; so after a rather fraught time in our lives." Nervous laughter rippled round the table, "Here we are again and, most importantly, our family is reconciled at last. Please everyone *do* enjoy the evening." She sat down to a round of applause and appreciative glances.

"I'll drink to that!" Horace announced.

Mrs Cross and Mrs Partridge entered the dining room with trays of smoked salmon terrine. Clare jumped up to help. Justyn rose to speak, but before doing so craned his neck, surreptitiously looking at the window, thinking he heard another noise. Pausing for a moment, with all eyes on him, he decided to ignore it again.

"Ladies and gentlemen of the jury," he started, to muffled laughter, "I have an announcement to make. After twenty years of tangled relations, romantic highlights and a few, ahem, interruptions, Clare and I have some news!"

Silence replaced the rattle of cutlery on plates. The convivial chatter abruptly stopped. He saw Pat holding her breath. "And that is … " he teased, "we're engaged to be married!" Spontaneous clapping mingled with shrieks of delight filled the huge dining room. Justyn, basking in the glory of Clare's smile, reciprocated it warmly. "And," he added, raising his voice above the applause, "we can give you the wedding date, August 5th next year, 12 noon, to be sort of precise!"

"Darling, you finally got him!" Pat jumped up and hugged Clare, with her eyes closed. She opened them, delighted to see Alison beaming at her. Horace was on his feet too, proposing a toast. His usual bombastic manner was back, replacing his earlier foul mood on discovering that he and Annabel had been put in the annexe, an outbuilding opposite the kitchen.

"Well, it's a shame you're not taking the nuptials after the glorious twelfth, we could have celebrated with the grouse!" Nobody took any notice, but Clare, for one, was happy to see her brother in better heart. They enjoyed a convivial meal. Soon Horace was seen lighting a large Cuban cigar while walking towards the billiards room with Danny, Oliver and Martin Whitlock in his wake.

"And just where do you think you're going?" Justyn stopped them in their tracks, instructing them to follow him to the kitchen to assist the women in clearing up. "This isn't the eighteenth century you know!"

Later, before retiring, Danny and Oliver couldn't resist horsing around with the suit of armour in the Great Hall. Danny removed the sinister looking sword from it's sheath and announced, "Christ, you could do some serious damage with this! Pat told me she took it out of storage, to have it cleaned." He bade them goodnight. Justyn frowned. For some reason the sword made him feel uneasy and he wished it wasn't there. As he walked up the stairs he pulled his phone out of his pocket. He needed to make an important call.

★★★★★

Justyn woke up to see Clare by the door.

"Where're you going?" Lifting his head, he saw her turning the handle.

"Sorry, darling. I thought you were asleep. I'm just popping down to put some things by the fire for Father Christmas."

"What? It's nearly 3 a.m. There aren't any children in the house. Why are you doing it? Come on, get back into bed, it's bloody freezing in this place!"

"Won't be long – family tradition …" She slipped on her dressing gown and closed the door behind her. As she walked along the landing towards the grand staircase with only her phone to light the way, she, noticed, almost for the first time the portrait of her grandfather. It was hanging where it had always been, at the top of the stairs. He was seated, wearing a lounge suit, a brandy glass in one hand and a cigar in the other. His gaze was enigmatic; his penetrating blue eyes fixed on a point beyond the viewer. As she looked more carefully there seemed to be an anger, an unease and perhaps a hint of insanity. She hurried down the stairs and ran across the cold hallway, her bare feet chilled by the marble floor.

The fetid aroma of Horace's cigars from earlier in the evening, hung heavy in the air. The hallway clock struck 3 a.m. She went over to the plastic bag she'd left on a side table earlier in the evening, and took out three carrots and a mince pie which she then carefully placed in front of the flickering fire. She enjoyed the warmth coming from it. It all felt so magical, that for a moment she actually believed Father Christmas *would* be coming to enjoy his mince pie.

She was shaken from her reverie when she noticed that the Christmas presents, which had been so neatly stacked under the Christmas tree, had been disturbed and when she looked more closely she saw that many of them had been unwrapped. She flicked the light switch on the wall, but the light didn't come on. She knew there must be some perfectly rational explanation for all this but even so felt a tremor of fear. A floorboard creaked but this was an old house which often rattled and sighed, so she tried to retain her composure. As she left the room she was brutally seized from behind and dragged backwards to the fireplace.

Concerned at the time she was taking, Justyn got out of bed, and wrapped himself in his dressing gown. He banged on Danny and Oliver's door as he hurried down the corridor. He had a feeling something was happening and feared it might be something bad.

"I know you're there, I know someone's there," he yelled. He flicked the light switch, the hall remained in darkness and a coldness enveloped him. He realised that someone had fused the lights. His mobile was on charge in the bedroom. All he could see were the glowing embers of the dying fire. Danny, having heard the commotion, appeared at his shoulder and held his mobile torch aloft, bellowing, "Who are you? What do you want?"

"What do I want?" It was the voice they had never wanted to hear again.

Leia joined them on the landing and called down:

"What do you want, Guy?" her voice was soothing and her words echoed down the stairs and across the Great Hall.

"What do I want?" repeated Guy in an even more sinister voice.

"Yes. What do I want, I wonder? I wonder? I haven't been given very much have I? Haven't had much, have I? You've all done rather nicely from the old man up there on the stairs, very nicely indeed. Still, some of the Christmas presents will come in handy, particularly as I had to leave all my worldly possessions in Spain. Not an easy business, faking suicide." Roope gave away his location by pointing his torch at the portrait of Ken Stone. Danny's phone torch found him. He was holding Clare in front of the huge Christmas tree. Roope had removed the sword from the suit of armour. The hilt was in his right hand while his left was wrapped tightly around Clare's mouth. She was struggling to speak.

"Okay, Guy. You're right. You have had a raw deal here. You've always had a raw deal. Let Clare go and we can sort things out." Justyn tried to arbitrate.

"Shut the fuck up, hippy boy…" Guy glared at him as Justyn boldly walked a few steps down the grand staircase towards him. "Back off now. One more step, hippy boy and your little lady's brown bread! Leia …" Guy addressed himself directly to her at the top of the stairs. "Leia, I've come here for you, I was looking for you. Let's leave all this behind. They don't care about you. They don't care about each other. They're not your friends, they're nobody's friends, they're only here because of the money." Guy didn't finish his sentence. A terrifying bang exploded inside the hall and screams rang out. Roope fell forward, crashing face down onto a Persian rug, rapidly saturating it with the blood pouring from his mouth. Such was the force of the blast that several pictures, including the portrait of Ken Stone, fell from their fixings, and clattered to the floor. All eyes turned to the source of the explosion. There stood Horace, proudly pulling himself up to his full height. He looked comical in a blue blazer, brightly emblazoned by a large gold crest on the front pocket, wearing it over his pyjamas. His shotgun was still smoking in his hand. Justyn rushed to Clare, who had collapsed on the floor. He helped her to her feet, thanking God that none of the shotgun pellets had hit her.

"Got the bastard!" Horace announced triumphantly, as if he'd just downed a stag. "We thought we heard some glass break, couldn't be sure, but then we heard all this commotion. Always thought Roope would turn up. Bad egg!"

Justyn stared at Horace. Did he understand what he'd just done? He rolled Roope over onto his back, checking he was really dead, before rolling him back again. Horace, the incorrigible buffoon, had just murdered someone, shot someone dead who had his back to him. Albeit someone who was threatening his sister and was on the run but questions would be asked and they would all be implicated. But all such concerns were lost on Horace.

"I'm going shooting on Boxing Day so I had my gun!" Horace was still milking the moment. Annabel tugged his jacket sleeve sharply, disturbed at seeing him so at ease, having just killed someone. They had been married for some twenty-odd years and sometimes she wondered if she really knew him at all.

CHAPTER FOURTEEN

Blue lights strafed the hedgerows as a succession of police vehicles drove at speed down the long drive to Stone Manor. As the fog lifted, the front lawns were flooded with light as powerful torches swept at the windows. The swift arrival of the police startled those inside. Had they been on Roope's trail? Roope's corpse lay prone on the floor, but no one admitted to dialling 999. As always, Justyn took charge, announcing he would answer the police questions. He unbolted several locks and yanked open the heavy, oak door.

First through it was Detective Inspector Linda Stobart. For a moment she wondered if she had interrupted a game of Murder Mystery, where each participant arrives with a part to play, well prepped and wearing the appropriate costume. But she soon saw the body, lying face down on the Persian carpet and realised that this was no game.

The huge Christmas tree made an incongruous backdrop. Her trained eye noticed the presents that had been opened in a rough and disrespectful way, many were scattered across the floor. As her eyes travelled across the group, she took stock of the terrified faces of the two elderly women.

"We had a call from the neighbours, alerting us to a disturbance they thought they had heard."

Scores of police swarmed into the house behind her. Danny's partner, Oliver, giggled nervously at the sudden surge of activity.

Danny felt anxious as he remembered how they had messed around with the suit of armour and the sword earlier in the evening, and how their fingerprints would be all over it.

"Yes, we've had a firearms tragedy, Inspector. We can explain everything. We've had a very narrow escape. It's been truly terrifying. This man, er, this man ..." Everyone's eyes followed Justyn's to the body, "is Guy Roope, he's a double murderer who the Spanish police had mistakingly informed us was dead." He noticed a wry expression on the Detective Inspector's face and worried for a moment that she might think he was making it up. "Long story short, he broke in and was holding Clare, here," he pointed to her, "hostage with this sword at her throat, threatening to kill her. We all knew he was quite capable of it." He bent down to pick up the sword to demonstrate the danger Clare had faced.

"Leave it!" Stobart instructed officiously, "it will be needed for fingerprinting."

Justyn blushed, knowing he was trying to exaggerate the threat Roope posed and feeling unsure of what approach the police might take. He was particularly concerned that Horace would face a serious grilling and if he gave silly or pompous answers the consequences could be serious.

Detective Inspector Linda Stobart formally introduced herself and her colleagues. Some dozen officers, with two sniffer dogs, dispersed and set about their work. The Christmas house guests – the cricket twelve, as Clare had christened them – were asked not to leave the hall; they chatted nervously while waiting to be questioned. The two aunts sat anxiously on a chaise longue, looking cold and frightened. Clare sat with them, reassuring them that the danger was over and that everything would be back to normal very soon. Her mother gripped her hand tightly as Clare stood up, having been granted permission to go and make them tea. Stopping at the doorway to the kitchen, she turned back to look at the two sisters, seeing clearly for the first time how severely traumatised they both looked. Aunt Alison's face, reddened by broken capillaries that spread from her cheeks to her ears, finally looked completely beaten. So many years of living a secret life of luxury at the expense of others had finally caught up with her. Alison stared briefly at her daughter, Sharon, before glancing across at Danny and then down at the floor.

The Detective Inspector explained that they would be setting up two incident rooms at the Manor, which would be dismantled when they left. They would then set up a permanent one at Ipswich police station. It was decided that the billiards room would make a 'display' room and the police constable in charge was to put items of evidence on the table. The first two items to be placed on the billiards table were the sword and a Smith and Wesson 45 handgun, retrieved from Roope's pocket. Justyn, barely containing his glee, shot a relieved look at Horace, knowing this could save the big oaf from a serious charge. It also bore witness to the horror they could all have been subjected to. No longer did Justyn feel he had exaggerated the threat they all faced. Horace, meanwhile, continued to look very pleased with himself.

The gun lay next to the sword and only Roope's fingerprints would be on both. At least, that was the case in Justyn's mind, but Danny knew otherwise. He knew his and Oliver's fingerprints would also be found on the sword. Next, they were surprised to see the police carrying a number of archive boxes, presumed to be from one of the police vehicles, which they were carrying into the display room.

"What on earth's in them?" Danny nervously whispered to Justyn, who shrugged nonchalantly. Horace grunted his irritation when an officer relieved him of his gun and took that too into the room. Each of the twelve took turns to be photographed. Photographs of the crime scene were quickly printed and pinned to a cork board.

The library was chosen for the interview room. The furniture was reconfigured with recording equipment rigged up for the interviews. Horace sighed noisily as he was called and led in,

"This is a bit over the top isn't it?" Facing three police officers, including Detective Inspector Stobart, Horace was his usual bombastic self, "Yes, I did shoot the bastard, and a bloody good job too. Saved a lot of bloodshed, could have been carnage, everyone here can vouch for that. Call them in!"

"We'll be calling them in, in our own good time!" After fielding a number of questions, Horace signed his statement with a melodramatic flourish.

Danny requested the aunts be interviewed next, pointing out that they had already suffered a terrible ordeal and it would be only kind to let them go to bed as soon as possible. Stobart was unmoved, staring back enigmatically, before replying; "No, they will not be next, in fact they will be last!" Appalled, Danny turned to Justyn for support, but was surprised when none was forthcoming.

"Oh, for goodness sake, show some compassion!" Horace's intervention was quickly rebuffed.

"You mind your own business. We decide the order of the interviews. You would do well to keep your mouth shut!" Annabel couldn't hold back a nervous giggle; the tension was getting to her, and she knew Horace would never be able to do that. "There are good reasons, which will become clear, why they …" the Detective Inspector turned to address the two old ladies, "will be last." The words hung in the air like a gathering storm. Clare looked quizzically at Justyn. Was there something else going on here? Justyn showed no reaction.

*****

At 5 a.m. they finally saw Detective Inspector Stobart and two colleagues leave the interview room with Alison Galvin. They waited anxiously. She had been with them far longer than any of the others. Several of the 'cricket twelve' exchanged glances, now suspecting something was up, something very serious.

"It's alright dears," Alison addressed them, her voice sounding other-worldly. Danny, was alarmed by his mother's state. "I don't need the handcuffs. I can't run anyway!" Alison laughed at her own joke. No one else did. Danny listened aghast to his mother's semi-delirious ramblings.

"What are you doing?" he shouted at the police, "Can't you see what a state she's in? She's a frail, old lady!"

"Calm down, darling, I knew this would happen one day ..." Justyn placed a restraining hand on Danny's shoulder. He tried to dart forward towards his mother, but was pulled back.

"We are arresting Mrs Alison Galvin on suspicion of conspiring, with two others, to the murder of Mr Hector Wallace on the night of August 23rd, 1972. We believe you were acting in concert with your late husband, Mr Paul Galvin, and your companion, now also deceased, Mr Don Davenport."

Detective Inspector Stobart's shrill tone shot through Danny like a dart.

"Just who are you?" he shouted.

"I have already told you, I'm Detective Inspector Linda Stobart. I'm from the Cornwall Constabulary and my team, the Devon and Cornwall Criminal Case Review Unit, arrived here tonight with the sole purpose of arresting your mother." Pat gasped, wondering how much more she could take.

"We informed our colleagues at Suffolk Constabulary yesterday that we were here to arrest Mrs Galvin before dawn. It was just an extraordinary coincidence that, just as we were closing in on solving a murder from forty-four years ago, another one occurred here tonight."

"Let her go!" shrieked Sharon Galvin, pointing at her mother. Danny leapt forward, holding her back. "Let her go. This happened so long ago, back in the 1970s, why dig around nearly half a century later?" she yelled.

"Just because it happened in the 1970s, it makes no difference. Your mother, Miss Galvin," the Detective Inspector turned to address her directly, "was involved in the cold brutal murder of an innocent man. It was a case …" her voice faltered, "a case that should have been prosecuted at the time."

Martin Whitlock muttered in Justyn's ear, "I think there's a personal agenda going on here."

"Sharon, we did arrange the murder of Hector Wallace. I'm sorry dear, but we did." Alison Galvin spoke clearly and calmly and then sat down to continue her story. "We had to silence him. Your father …" addressing both Danny and Sharon, "your father knew all about my relationship with Don Davenport, he would stay near us, over in Hayle. We would meet in St Ives, but never at the hotel. It was Don's idea, of course, he knew Father was a paedophile. Come on, Pat, you knew it too. Don had hired a private detective to track Father's behaviour, particularly with Hector Wallace. Anyway," Alison continued with new energy, "we discovered Hector was going to go to the police. Don had the evidence. We all knew if Hector spoke we'd never be able to blackmail father. Don said we had to deal with Hector."

"How much did Dad know? How involved was he?" Danny asked.

"He was persuaded, let's say. It took a bit of doing." Alison's cold, calculating words clearly revealed her now as someone who had been complicit in murder. She sounded as steely and indefensible as any other murderer. No one, not even her own children, sought to defend her now. "You see, because of his house building project in Penzance," she continued, as if this was something of historical interest, "he thought he was going to be ruined. He felt a terrible failure. In the end he knew blackmailing his father-in-law was his only way out, and probably a way of getting his own back a bit." She laughed again. No one else did. "He knew Hector was the one person who could ruin things."

"He also wanted to get Hector's potential inheritance," Justyn's interruption was cold and hard-edged. His need for justice for Hector was clear to all.

"Don used to say," Alison was oblivious to the interruption, "you know two can keep a secret providing one of them is dead." It was as if her recent transformation into a reformed person, had been simply an illusion. They all stared at her, contempt written on their faces.

"So, how did all this come out now? Why did the police re-open the case?" Martin Whitlock broke the silence.

"It was the fisherman," Alison resumed as if she was reading them a bedtime story, "you see we paid him, the fisherman, Trevor Mullings, to get Hector drunk and lead him out to the sea."

"Enough!" Justyn shouted. But she was determined to finish her story. Danny motioned to Justyn. He needed to hear it.

"You see, it was Trevor, after all these years, he told everything to the nice, young police lady here. Everyone thought he'd died, but no he hadn't." She half laughed; was insanity beginning to grip her? "We had to arrange for him to disappear. Don and Paul managed that. Apparently he'd always wanted to fish on the west coast of Ireland." Danny heard his mother out, feeling he was in a trance and realising there was no way he could even think of defending her now. He wanted his mother out of his sight right now. He never wanted to see her again. He put his arm around Sharon's shoulders. She leaned her head into his neck, sighing. They both watched their mother being led from the house that her father had built as a monument to his ego.

"I'm sorry darlings," she called out, "the sins of the past have caught up with me." She sounded almost relieved.

"Just one thing," Danny shouted after her. "Just one thing I want to know!" but the door had now closed. They would never see their mother again.

"And that is?" Justyn interrupted.

"Who told the police? I mean, who alerted them to Davenport? What led them to interview Mullings again? Why did they re-open the case after all this time?"

"I did." The voice was Justyn's. The others turned towards him, shocked. They barely noticed that the police had started dismantling the 'display' and 'interview' rooms.

As they filed out, Stobart addressed the group again.

"I don't imagine any of you have endured a night like this before, and hopefully never will again, especially the night before Christmas. But you can rest easy now the killer is dead." Roope's shattered body had long since been removed, "And for myself and my team, we have closure on something that should have been resolved a very long time ago. Happy Christmas!"

Nobody responded.

★★★★★

"How did you know?"

Justyn smirked. He was waiting for this.

"I'd pieced it together, Danny. A few nights before Hector was murdered, he told me all about the abuse he'd suffered at the hands of your grandfather."

Clare looked concerned. Was the only man she had ever truly loved about to reveal something further, which might even threaten their relationship?

"We were in the hotel in St Ives, in August 1972; it was late, probably gone 2 a.m. I'd been in the pub band that night and helped escort Hector back to the hotel. He was seven sheets to the wind, but not so bad that he was insensible. Tom Youlen, the night porter, had fetched us tea and …" Justyn sighed as if about to release himself from some terrible burden.

"Are you sure you want to continue?" Pat asked, weary from so much trauma and lack of sleep. She feared for her daughter's future happiness.

"I'm sorry, Pat, I understand your concern but you must all hear me out. Hector was only thirteen when he went to work for Ken Stone, as an apprentice in his landscape gardening business. Almost from the start, Stone abused him," he looked around anxiously, aware of the discomfort he was now causing. "And please don't anyone give me the, oh, it was the 1970s. Abuse is abuse, even if the person who perpetrated it is now dead." Justyn's attention was taken by Whitlock escorting Monika up the stairs. She made no comment, but stiffened as she moved. It made Justyn feel uncomfortable, but he continued: "Hector told Tom, the night porter and me how Stone ruined his life, took away his self-esteem and drove him to drink. When it emerged that Stone had been blackmailed, directing all his wealth to Alison, and by association, Davenport, I knew then she must have been involved in getting Hector out of the way. It didn't take much to suspect that Paul was involved in it." Justyn chose his words carefully, not referring to Paul as Danny and Sharon's father.

"Just think about if for a moment. All three select the same place to disappear to – Mallorca – could it really just be about the money? No, it could not, money alone is very unlikely to cause people to disappear, deceive their loved ones, go into hiding or fake death and re-invent themselves. They had to disappear, and in Paul Galvin's case, change his identity and fake his own death, because they were all involved in murder. So, there we have it, a massive fraud on the rest of the family and a tragic end to a life." Justyn's eyes welled up. "Hector was a friend of mine, a very special person who didn't have a bad bone in his body."

He turned to Clare, wondering how she was taking this, when he saw the kitchen door open to reveal Detective Inspector Stobart walking into the Great Hall.

"I stayed around. It's an old policing trick I learnt from my father. He told me it was always a good plan to have one police officer remain at a crime scene, when everyone thinks we have gone," she smiled weakly. "Never know what might be revealed when everyone thinks we've gone home." Most of the group now looked exhausted, unsure they could face anymore. "But I have a question for you, Justyn."

"Yes?"

"How did you know Davenport was involved?" Before he could answer, she continued: "Mrs Galvin confirmed it to us, in her confession tonight, but I'm interested, how did you know?"

"It's on the DVD, the cine-film my brother took that last night in Cornwall. Danny has it on his laptop. It shows a group of us in the pub, dated 23rd August 1972."

Danny took a step forward guessing what he was about to hear. It didn't take Justyn long.

"There he was, Don Davenport, talking to Paul Galvin. If you examine it, you can even see them looking directly at Hector as they spoke. They dismissed him as a hopeless drunk, and they hatched their plan. He was ..."

"Leave it!" Danny cried.

"Expendable." Justyn ignored him. Danny had now lost his last card, the one that he had hoped would tell him his father was innocent. Throughout all the evening's tribulations and revelations, Danny had clung to the hope that his father might just be innocent. That it would all be down to his mother and Davenport. "So Hector," Justyn concluded, "we have justice for you at last."

"Why did you care so much about this cold case?" Danny directed his question not at Justyn, but at Stobart.

"It's what the Devon and Cornwall Criminal Cases Review does," she replied somewhat glibly.

"Yes, of course, but this goes beyond that, doesn't it? You've got something else going on here haven't you? You've been on a crusade haven't you?"

Stobart looked at Danny, then at the others. She counted: now there were eight, the original twelve were minus Alison, who was in police custody, Monika who had retired to her room with Martin Whitlock and Annabel, Horace's wife, had slunk off when no one was looking. The detective's eyes scanned the room once more. Justyn was standing near Clare, who was still cradling Leia as if she was her child. Pat, looking dejected on the chaise longue was being comforted by her son. Danny and Oliver were sitting on the table. Finally she looked at Sharon who was utterly distraught with a wild look in her eyes.

"There is a reason," Stobart finally spoke. She started to falter. They all looked on, astonished. "You see, my father, PC Gary Stobart, was one of the investigating officers in 1972. He and his superior officer, Detective Inspector Roy Higham, were suspended from the force after the case collapsed. Their Superintendent deemed it had been bungled and they weren't fit to wear the badge. Of course it wasn't really like that was it Justyn? Danny?" She stared at them knowing they were in Cornwall at the time and that both would remember the case.

"There were dark forces at work, for sure." Justyn replied, trying to guess what she was getting at. "There was one rather influential man who seemed able to get the case closed very quickly."

Justyn knew he was out of his depth. Stobart took over: "The CPS were pretty quick to close the case; suspicions pointed at the cardiologist, Richard Hughes-Webb, the person Justyn's alluding to, who appeared responsible for having the case closed. He'd been a suspect. He'd kept poison in his nearby holiday home and Tom, the night porter, looked after it for him. Then Tom accidentally poisoned himself with it, and days later Hector was found drowned. No prosecutions were forthcoming. The coroner ruled accidental death for both. My father was never reinstated, neither was his superior, Roy Higham, but Higham didn't mind. He didn't mind because he was now a very wealthy man, living in Spain. Now I wonder how that could have happened, wasn't that strange?" She paused for breath, "It happened, of course because he was bent, and his Superintendent was very happy too. Guess what? He had also been nobbled, but not by Hughes-Webb, neither of them had been. Hughes-Webb was, in fact, an honourable man."

This was massively significant for Danny. Hughes-Webb's daughter Suzie's suicide, was all too fresh in his mind. They had been very close. It had happened only last year. To think Hughes-Webb was innocent all along of conspiring to murder and of paying off the police, brought tears to his eyes. Suzie had committed suicide because her father's reputation was in tatters, and it turned out he had done nothing wrong. Never a day had passed since, when Danny hadn't thought of Suzie.

"So, you now have justice for your father, Detective Inspector?"

"Wish I could have achieved it in his lifetime, but he died a broken man a long time ago. After he left the force, he worked as a coal delivery man at Redruth, but after that he abandoned my mother and then drifted. I was sixteen when we had a visit from a former colleague in the force telling us that he'd died."

"How did he die?"

"He was found washed up on the beach at Carbis Bay."

Justyn rose to his feet and placed his arm around the police officer. She didn't push him away, but began to cry uncontrollably.

"Well, it's been a helluva night and I think it's time we drew stumps," Horace announced.

DI Stobart, ignored him: "You should all know Justyn alerted me to where you all would be, particularly Mrs Galvin. It was time to make our move and arrest her. We had an arrangement that we would swoop when Justyn phoned to tell us everyone was in bed."

"So, the bit about the neighbour reporting a disturbance was all made up?" Stobart looked coy.

"One final thing?" Danny addressed his question directly to her.

"Who paid off the police, back in 1972?" He closed his eyes, hoping the next words he heard would be the name Don Davenport, but, after a brief pause, he heard the two words he most dreaded:

"Paul Galvin."

Danny turned to Justyn for support, but was shocked to be rebuffed by a wave of his hand. There was a hard, uncompromising look on Justyn's face.

*****

The grandfather clock struck 6 a.m. and night was turning towards day. All the police had left; there was a listless atmosphere and a feeling that not everything had been resolved. Although they were all exhausted no one wanted to be the first to go to bed. Justyn broke the silence.

"We need Martin Whitlock down here, with Monika." There was no mistaking the edge to Justyn's voice. "Horace, you're not involved further, you can go. Please take your mother, she has suffered enough. Can you ask Monika and Martin to come down?"

Pat, escorted by Horace, trudged slowly up the stairs, so exhausted, that even the effort of turning her head back to acknowledge him was beyond her.

"Oliver and Sharon, please go too. The rest of you must stay." He knew exactly who he wanted to remain and why. There was no mistaking the intent in Justyn's voice and manner.

Justyn put on his glasses and thumped the case down on the table in front of him. "We need Whitlock and Monika, now!" His anger startled them.

Eventually Martin and Monika appeared. They were sleepy and dishevilled and looked like two naughty children in front of the headmaster.

"Will you both take a seat?" Justyn was temporarily shocked when he caught sight of himself in the mirror. His long white hair was cruelly receding, and his white beard looked thin and scraggy. Danny sat expressionless on his left. Next to him sat Leia with Clare, on Justyn's right, her arms folded. Whitlock gave a contemptuous shrug as he sat down opposite Justyn; Monika picked her way round the table to sit next to him. Justyn drew a deep breath.

"So, tell us, what *did* happen to Grant Morrison? Monika?" Whitlock let out a hoot of derisive laughter. Monika blushed, horrified he'd directed the question at her.

"We don't know,"

"Okay, Monika, let's put it this way, Grant didn't die in a traffic accident did he? So are you going to be a good girl and tell us what really happened, before you get *your* fucking collar felt?" Whitlock flew out of his chair and lunged at Justyn.

"No, darling, no!" yelled Monika. Justyn jumped to his feet, lifting his arms in self-defence.

"Sit down Martin!" Justyn's bellowed command stopped Whitlock in his tracks. He sat down. "We need answers NOW!" Justyn shifted his eyes from Whitlock to Monika, then to Danny and Clare. He could almost taste their bewilderment. He turned to Leia. "It turns out there was another reason why Grant was in Mallorca."

"What was it?" Leia couldn't imagine why this would concern her.

"Let me explain." Justyn leaned forward in his chair and his tone softened. "You see, after Grant died his wife, Brigit asked me to collect his things from the hotel – funnily enough the hotel where you work Leia – and among them was a huge collection of papers – an old diary, letters, documents, bits of paper. I put them away in the hotel to keep them safe and didn't look at them until I got home. I'm sure, in the end, Grant would have wanted me to know what he'd been doing. I suspect he just wanted to keep quiet about it until he had something to tell us."

"The suspense is killing me." said Danny, "get on with it."

"It turns out that he'd been doing research on your mother, Leia, and had managed to find out what had happened to you after she died. He was so *very* close to finding you."

"And …?" Leia shot a glance at Monika, who shrugged indifferently.

"He was looking for *you*, Leia." Justyn let the words hang. Leia stared at him.

"Leia. He was your father!" Leia gasped. Monika looked down at the table.

"Are you mad?" As Whitlock spoke, he craned his neck round to look at the heavy, oak front door behind him. Justyn anticipated his next move.

"Stay where you are!" Whitlock glared back. "Stay where you are, Martin, I think it's time, don't you, that Monika told us what really happened on Grant's last journey? We know the roads are dangerous, accidents can happen, but that's not it, that's not what happened, is it, Monika?" Justyn folded his arms, sat back, and waited. Whitlock jerked his chair back and jumped to his feet.

"I said stay where you are!"

Whitlock glanced at the door that led to the kitchen and then outside but before he could make a move he saw the door open a little. Slowly it dawned on him, someone was there; "We're not alone are we?" Whitlock asked uncomfortably. Monika shook her head.

"No, Martin, we're not alone and I think you and Monika both know why."

Whitlock heard the floorboard creak behind the kitchen door, watching as it was very gently nudged a little further open. "Has someone called the police back?" Whitlock was losing his nerve. Justyn ignored the question.

"Isn't it time you told us how you were involved with Andrzej's gang and how they forced Grant off the road, Monika? I think you owe it to Leia to explain what happened to her father."

"You bitch!" Leia screamed, lunging at Monika. "Why?" Danny and Justyn leapt up to restrain her. "Why did you kill my … my father?" Leia broke down, collapsing on the floor, howling. Clare rushed to try to lift her, wrapping an arm underneath her.

"We need answers, Monika."

"I … I not have easy life, not like you all have, things not easy for me. When I was child I knew Andrzej, he my brother's friend – he strong, everyone looked up to Andrzej and he always have gang. He came back home to Warsaw, one time, and told me if I go to Mallorca I get plenty money and easy life – all I have to do is, he say, 'honey trap'. I think if I make money then I come back to Warsaw and apply to music academy. I always dreamed of play music." She paused, hoping for sympathy.

"Yes, alright Monika, but what happened when you went to Mallorca?"

"When I'm there he takes me to place where I can meet Mr Galvin, a fancy restaurant in Deià. I work as waitress and one day ..." she shot a glance at Danny. "You see ..."

"No, Monika!" Whitlock yelled.

"Yes ... yes, Martin, I must say now. Mr Galvin, er, Peter, as I called him, had much money and soon I hear about Mrs Galvin and Mr Davenport." Whitlock looked appalled, knowing all hope was gone.

"The trouble start when the café man, owner, in Palma Nova, tell Andrzej that Grant is looking for Mrs Galvin. Andrzej thinks he must be stopped, he must be silenced, he says maybe we arrange an accident." She looked around, nervously wondering if they understood. Whitlock shook his head.

"Yes. Don't worry, we know what you mean. So who was in the car that drove at Grant?"

Whitlock jumped up again and placed his hand firmly over Monika's mouth. Monika pushed it away.

"Martin, I can't lie anymore, neither should you. Andrzej and me were in car!" she blurted out.

Leia picked up a heavy glass ashtray and hurled it at her. It caught Monika's forehead and she fell backwards and crashed to the floor. Whitlock was quickly at her side.

*****

"There, there," Clare soothed Leia, "don't talk, darling." Leia's mascara flowed with her tears down her face.

Danny glared at Whitlock. "Now, Martin, I think it's time *you* answered some questions."

"Oh yes. What about, Danny?"

Whitlock coldly held Danny's stare.

"About the money. Sharon and my inheritance from our father's will!" His voice was harsh, unyielding.

"Um …"

"Probate came through a week ago, why haven't you distributed the funds? Why the delay?"

"Well, you see, there's been a wrinkle, a problem I didn't foresee." Whitlock hesitated, running his fingers through his hair. He took some papers from his inside pocket, "You see, Danny, I found these at your father's house. It's his last will, formally prepared and witnessed by another solicitor in Sóller." Danny's eyes narrowed, he'd been half expecting this.

"Well, there's a thing!"

"Do you mind if I take Leia upstairs, she's very distressed – unless, of course, there's anything else you've got up your sleeve for us tonight, JS?" Clare's interruption induced a faint smile from Justyn. He jumped up to kiss her, holding her tight.

"I'm sorry, Clarezy, I've got to stay with Danny, " he whispered in her ear. She smiled, feeling a little more secure, hoping their union might yet survive the turmoil of the night. Danny watched Clare and Leia climb the stairs until they were out of sight.

"Okay, Martin, what are you saying, what does this new will mean?"

"Well ..." Whitlock cleared his throat and placed his hands in front of him on the table. "The new will is legal so we have no choice but to adopt it." He barely bothered to disguise his excitement at the prospect.

"So, who might the beneficiaries be now, I wonder? Who's the lucky winner of thirty three million pounds?" Danny took a menacing step towards Whitlock.

"Well, it's a little awkward, Danny, but your father ultimately left what's left of his one third share of the hundred million pounds to Monika."

"And now Monika's almost certainly going down, on a murder charge. Go on, amaze us some more, tell us you have her Power of Attorney if by any chance she can't look after her own affairs?"

"Well, yes, as a matter of fact, I do."

Danny, grabbed the will, studying it quickly.

"That's not my father's signature! You've forged it, you lying bastard."

"No, Danny, you're mistaken, I can show you this is his signature, it's consistent with other documents. You hadn't seen him for a long time, signatures change."

"No one's going to believe you, you're a pathological liar!" Danny and Whitlock were squaring up to each other when Danny suddenly struck him full in the face with his fist; Whitlock recovered, raining hard punches back, forcing Danny onto his knees. Justyn rushed to his aid but Whitlock made a dash for the kitchen door, where Horace's clenched fist was waiting for him. Whitlock fell, cracked his head on the corner of the skirting board and passed out with blood streaming from a wound on the back of his head.

"Oh my God, Horace, what have you done?" Justyn quickly examined the stricken Whitlock.

"Danny, he's breathing, he's got a pulse, get an ambulance, quick, and call the police!"

*****

Justyn and Danny stood motionless, side by side with the police, watching the paramedics lift Whitlock onto a stretcher. After a short interrogation and on the strength of Justyn, Danny and Horace's statements, the police arrested Monika and the prostrate Whitlock on suspicion of being involved in the murder of Grant Morrison. The police took Monika with them and followed the ambulance down the long drive and ultimately back to Ipswich.

Justyn shrugged, before shaking his head. "God. What a night!"

"You could say that!" Danny responded.

"Well, at least they think he'll live, a broken jaw and a cut below the eye won't take him to heaven!"

"He could go to hell in a handcart for all I care!" Horace announced, carrying coffees for the other two.

"You realise, Horace, you could have been on a double murder charge tonight."

"Piffle! I rescued you all from Roope and Whitlock deserved a proper sorting out, trying to swindle you and Sharon and the rest of us."

"The rest of us?" Danny was taken aback.

"Oh yes," continued Horace, "well, Aunt Alison and Davenport's share got split between us all, so should Uncle Paul's. After all, it all came from Grandpa Stone, so it should be shared out evenly!"

"Can you come?" Clare yelled down the stairs. "It's Leia. She's hysterical." Justyn raced up, two at a time, hastily following Clare into their room.

"Please help me! I need to know more about my father. Why did he abandon us? Why did he take so long to come and find me? It's all too much to take in." Leia was confused and tearful.

"I don't know, Leia. I really don't. I'm sure he felt very bad about it. He never confided in me, but Grant was a good man. From what I have found out it seems he just took fright. He was young and immature and had a promising legal career in front of him. I honestly don't think he was strong enough to throw it all in and live here, no matter how much he wanted to. And then of course he got married. I have no idea whether his wife knows. But don't let's worry about any of that now. It's Okay Leia." He took her left arm in his hand, patting it, soothing her.

"Yes." She gulped, trying to ease her breathing.

Justyn slowly released his grip, placing her arm back on the bed. He paced the room, thinking carefully as he spoke:

"I wanted to share all this with you in person when the time was right, not like this, amid all this chaos and trauma. I'm so sorry you had to find out like this."

"Please can you describe him?" Justyn did better than that. He took out his mobile phone and scrolled to a photograph of Grant.

"This was taken quite recently at a wedding."

Leia, exhausted and tearful, gazed at the smiling figure leaning on a chair and holding a glass of champagne.

"Yes, that's him. I remember him in the hotel. How funny. I was concerned that he'd left without paying. There was something about him. So, he was looking for *me*! And we look so alike. I have his eyes!"

Clare gently held Leia's face in her hands and looked into her eyes.

"Yes … yes, you certainly have … and now Leia, Justyn and I have decided you are coming to live with us. We'll look after you. It's the least we can do for you." Leia beamed.

"And for Grant." Justyn added.

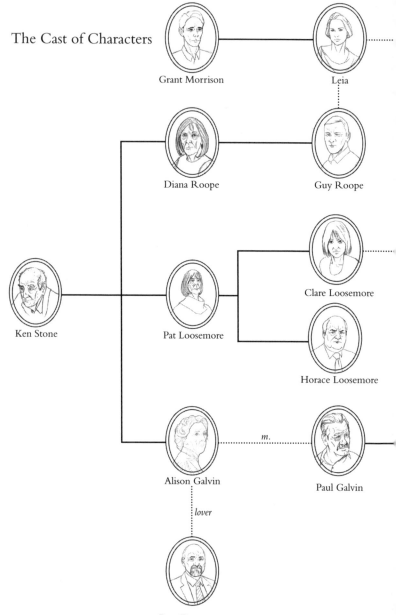

The Cast of Characters

Grant Morrison

Leia

Diana Roope

Guy Roope

Clare Loosemore

Ken Stone

Pat Loosemore

Horace Loosemore

m.

Alison Galvin

Paul Galvin

lover

Don Davenport

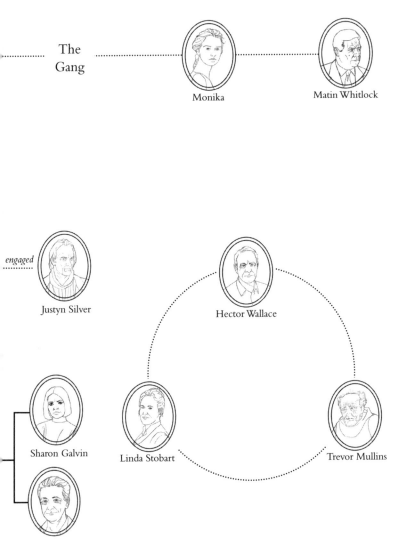

The Gang

Monika

Matin Whitlock

engaged

Justyn Silver

Hector Wallace

Sharon Galvin

Linda Stobart

Trevor Mullins

Danny Galvin